Flight

By Alyssa Rose Ivy

Cover Design: Phatpuppyart.com

Editing: Stephanie T. Lott A.K.A. Bibliophile

Proofreading: Kris Kendall

ISBN-13: 978-1478292845

ISBN-10: 1478292849

To Kristen, the co-pilot on all of my YA adventures.

Acknowledgements

This book would not have been possible without the support of my family. Thank you especially to Grant for your constant encouragement and faith in my writing. Thanks to Jennifer Snyder for your feedback, friendship, and for making this journey of writing books even more enjoyable. Thanks to Christina Ahn Hickey for the helpful early feedback. Last but certainly not least, a huge thank you to all of my readers for giving me the opportunity to share my stories with you.

Preface

Closing my eyes, I tried to block it all out. Convinced I was about to die, I was only partly aware of his arms around me.

"You said you wanted an adventure," he said quietly, teasingly, as he tightened his hold.

My stomach dropped out as an intense and complete feeling of weightlessness engulfed me. The wind stung my face as memories flooded my mind. I thought of my parents, of all the things I wanted to tell them but never did, my friends from home, and the experiences I longed for. Quickly my thoughts changed to more recent memories, to Levi.

"Open your eyes," he whispered, somehow knowing my eyes were clenched shut.

Against my better judgment, I listened. The scream died in my throat as we hurtled toward the water that had seemed so beautiful from the roof above.

One

I'd sworn off men, or really boys, because those were the only type of males I tended to attract. The numbers on the pump moved painfully slow as I reminded myself of the decision. Tying my hair up in a knot on the top of my head, I struggled to save my neck from the heat created by my long brown hair. Even a ponytail wasn't enough for the Mississippi heat. I had heard all about the hot summers of the south, but I didn't expect the temperatures to be quite so scorching in June. I was terrified to think about what August would feel like.

Finally finished with the gas, I got back in the car to wait impatiently for my best friend Jess. We were only a few hours away from New Orleans, but after two days of driving, every minute was torture. I started the engine and turned the AC on high before leaning back into the comfortable seat. The new car smell still permeated my Land Rover, an over the top high school graduation gift from my father. I loved it and appreciated the gift but wished my dad had checked with me before special ordering it in what he believed was my favorite color—lavender. I didn't have the heart to tell him that purple had stopped being my favorite when I was five.

After a few minutes, Jess slid into the passenger seat. "Want some chips or soda?" she asked while smoothing out her blond hair, putting a few strands back in place behind her ear. The effort was wasted. Her hair was still messy and matched the flushed expression she wore.

"Please tell me you didn't make out with someone to get free chips." I rolled my eyes hoping she would surprise me just this once by not having done it. We had been best friends since the sixth grade, and she had been boy crazy the whole time I'd known her.

"I didn't make out with him for the chips; I did it because he was hot."

Stifling a laugh, I pulled back out onto the road toward I-59. "Sure."

"We're only young once. Don't be so uptight." Jess snapped her gum loudly.

"Hey, it's fine, but don't come complaining to me when you get some weird communicable disease from one of the random guys you hook up with."

"Allie, I love you, but you have to relax. Promise me you'll at least try to have fun this summer." She sighed dramatically.

"I'll try," I said with exaggerated frustration. I planned to have a great summer, just one that didn't involve guys.

"That's not good enough. You're not going to let Toby ruin the entire summer are you? So you dated a jerk, who cares, forget about him."

"I'm not going to let Toby ruin anything. I'm the one who dumped him, remember?" Thinking about Toby threatened to put me in a worse mood. He had only been the latest in a string of

2

disappointing dating experiences. First there was Steve, we broke up when I found him cheating on me—with my best guy friend. After that was Matthew, who took commitment phobia to a whole new level when he actually set a cap on how often I could text message him. With Toby it wasn't anything dramatic, the romance just didn't live up to my expectations. Somehow, his declarations of how great of a power couple we would make didn't cut it. As relieved as I was about avoiding him all summer, I still had to deal with him at Princeton in the fall.

"So does that mean you're ready to move on?" Jess asked excitedly.

"No. I told you, I've sworn off men."

"Sweetheart, you do realize that men have many valuable roles other than boyfriends, right? Instead, how about you swear off boyfriends and just have fun?"

"I don't care what you do with guys, but I am never going to be the girl that just hooks up, okay?"

"We'll see about that."

Wanting to avoid a fight, I decided to ignore her last comment. Sometimes it was easier to let her think she won.

When I didn't answer, she decided to continue. "Maybe getting away from high school boys will help."

"Maybe," I mumbled under my breath.

She appeared not to hear me and changed the subject. "It was so cool of your dad to let us come down and hang out at the hotel all summer!"

"You mean it was cool of him to give us jobs, right?" I tried to keep a straight face, but really, I wasn't surprised by her choice of words. When Dad called to ask if I wanted to work at a hotel he had recently purchased in New Orleans, I agreed only if Jess could come with me. She wouldn't be much use as a coworker but she did have the ability to make any situation fun. I was counting on her working her magic.

***

The Crescent City Hotel looked exactly as I expected; a historic building complete with wrought iron balconies and the dangling ferns that were in every picture I had seen of the French Quarter. Following along with the GPS, I turned onto Royal Street and pulled up front to the valet, not sure where I was supposed to park. Before I could worry for long, my dad knocked on the window.

He opened the door once I unlocked it, taking my hand to help me out. "Hey sweetie, how was the trip?" He pulled me into a hug as soon as my feet hit the pavement. If you didn't know any better you'd think we had a normal father-daughter relationship.

"It was fine, we made great time."

"Hi Mr. Davis!" Jess yelled as she ran around the car.

"Hi Jessica, I'm so glad you were able to come down with my Allie."

"Of course! Thanks again for the job!"

"It's my pleasure; I hope you girls have a nice time." He caught my eye over Jess's head. Even as little as he knew Jess, he was under no misconceptions about her work ethic.

Dad glanced behind him, lifting a finger and a bellhop a little older than us started unloading bags from the back of the car. Before he had finished moving our bags to the cart, Jess was already chatting him up. With my dad watching, the poor guy was trying to stay professional.

"Let's go Jess." I grabbed her arm and led her inside. Dad had already gone ahead.

The lobby felt huge, much larger than it looked from the outside. All the money my dad had poured into the updates showed. Large travertine tiles covered the floor and dark wainscoting framed the room, while a beautiful chandelier with dangling crystals helped light the space. The etched glass in the sidewall that bore the name of the hotel typified the way he had modernized the hotel without losing all its historical character. I especially loved the solid mahogany bar. I'd like to say my dad had an eye for design, but I'm sure he had nothing to do with the selections. The fact that he was even at the hotel was surprising. He usually oversaw his properties from afar.

Looking up from the bar, I locked eyes with an incredibly hot guy. At over six feet tall with brown hair and wearing a tight shirt that barely concealed his muscular arms and chest, it would have been impossible not to notice him. He smiled at me and I found myself smiling back before I snapped myself out of it. Ignoring the invitation in his smile I quickly looked away. "You swore off men," I reminded myself.

"Do you girls want to see your room or get some lunch first?" my dad asked, relieving me of my thoughts about the guy.

"See our room," I answered quickly. "Is that okay, Jess?"

"Yeah, sure," she said distantly. I didn't bother looking, assuming she had found the same distraction.

My dad laughed as he led us to the elevators. "I put you girls in a suite on the top floor."

The elevator reached our floor and we walked toward our room. It came as no surprise, but our suite was luxurious. Jess and I each had our own room with a bathroom and we shared a large common living space complete with a kitchenette. Two French doors in the main living area opened out onto a balcony overlooking the street below.

"Wow Dad, you really didn't need to give us this suite for the whole summer."

"Of course I did. I'm your father. Now, why don't you girls get yourself settled and meet me in the courtyard for lunch in about a half hour?"

"Sounds great," I answered.

As soon as the door clicked Jess gave me a knowing smile. "So, uh, I thought you were swearing off guys."

"I am," I said defensively. Damn, she must have caught me eyeing him.

"Don't try to deny it. I saw you checking out that guy and he was checking you out too by the way. Totally hot, but I'll let you have him, his other friends were cute too."

"Don't even start." My response was automatic but inside I was surprised I hadn't even noticed his friends.

"Oh, come on, promise me that if he's still there you'll go talk to him," Jess pushed.

"No way."

"Why not?" she asked.

"Because I'm not interested, end of story."

"Oh no, you aren't getting off that easily."

Thankfully, I was saved from further argument by a knock. The bellboy from outside had arrived with our bags. He unloaded them two at a time, leaving them just inside the door.

"Do you girls need anything else?" Without my dad's presence he seemed much more interested in talking.

"I think we're all set for now, but we might need something later." Jess had turned on the charm.

"Oh yeah? Maybe I should give you my number then. I'm Billy by the way."

7

I tuned out their conversation, grabbing one of my bags to move it into my bedroom. Shaking my head, I laughed. I had to admit the bellboy was cute; he had the blond surfer boy look going for him, but leave it to Jess to get a phone number a few minutes after arriving in a city.

I heard the door click closed moments before Jess bounded into my room.

"Oh my god, this is going to be an awesome summer." She sprawled out on my bed.

"Hey Jess?"

"Yeah?"

"Don't ever change, okay?" I laughed.

"Are you making fun of me?" She sat up indignantly.

"Not at all. I just know I'm going to miss you this year."

"Aww, I'll miss you too. But we'll only be a train ride apart." She was going to her dream school, NYU.

"I know."

"And you could have gone to school in the city. You're the one who wanted to head to Jersey."

"Yeah, because Princeton is really settling, huh?"

"It is when you are only going there because your parents want you to."

I brushed it off, unwilling to let her know how much the jab hurt. "Let's go meet my dad; I'm starving." I headed to the door before Jess could argue. I'd never told her how I'd actually wanted to go somewhere more urban for school. Either she was more perceptive than I thought, or I was more transparent.

My eyes drifted to the bar as we walked through the lobby to the restaurant. I sighed with relief, but couldn't help but feel some disappointment as I noticed the now empty bar area.

"I guess you're off the hook for now, but next time you won't be so lucky," Jess said as she noticed the expression on my face.

I didn't even answer.

Two

As soon as we walked into the courtyard, Dad waved us over to a table. The umbrella beckoned, as I already felt myself sweating from the thick humid heat. Jess linked her arm with mine as we headed over to the table.

"Get much unpacking done?" Dad asked as soon as we were all seated.

"I did, not so much Jess."

"Were you too distracted Jessica?" Dad asked with a wry smile.

"What do you mean?"

"I'm not that old you know. You think I didn't notice the way you and that young man were looking at each other? I happen to know he took your bags upstairs."

Jess's cheeks took on an uncharacteristic blush. "Oh, yeah. Billy seems pretty cool."

"Thought so. Just be careful, he's quite a few years older than you are."

"Dad, stop."

"Her father isn't here; I have to at least try to provide some semblance of parental authority." He leaned back in his chair.

"Because you know so much about parental authority…?" I trailed off. Dad's glare told me I was about to cross a line.

"Speaking of parents, Allie, I had a little chat with the father of a friend of yours." I didn't like the expression he wore. Something bad was coming.

"You actually know some of my friend's parents?" Cranky from the drive I wasn't holding back.

"Yes, Tyler Henderson told me something interesting." He searched my face.

"And what did Mr. Henderson have to say?" I groaned. Toby must have gone crying to his dad.

"He told me you and Toby were experiencing some sort of misunderstanding."

"A misunderstanding?"

"Yes. I let him know that I thought the two of you were old enough to work out your problems yourself. " Dad smiled.

"I can't believe his dad called you. But be honest, did you even know Toby and I were dating?"

"Hey, give credit where credit is due. I know more about your life than you think."

"You've seen me twice in the last year. You barely ever come home to visit anymore." I tried not to let it get to me too much, but he'd always made it clear that Westchester, even with me there, was the last place he wanted to be.

"True, but we video chat once a week, I thought you liked that."

Jess laughed. "You Skype Mr. Davis?"

"First, Allie accuses me of not knowing anything about her life, now you think I'm

11

incapable of using basic technologies. You ladies are hard to dine with. But, we're together now, Allie, isn't that what matters?"

"So does that mean you'll be sticking around this summer?" I took a sip of water, already sure of his response.

"I will be in and out. I'll try to be around as much as possible, but you know travel is part of my business. One of the reasons I invited you down here was to introduce you to that business. You need to start getting your feet wet; this is going to be your company one day."

Words sat on the tip of my tongue, but I couldn't let them out. I wanted to tell him that I didn't want his business, but that was a fight for another day.

He took advantage of my silence. "Are you going to tell me what happened with Toby?"

"Nothing happened, it just didn't work out."

"That's it? That's all you're going to give me? Jessica, a little help here?"

"Sorry, I am so not getting in the middle of this." Jess held up her hands in defense.

"Can we please change the subject?"

"We can, once you tell me what happened." He swirled around the ice in his glass as though he had all the time in the world. I knew otherwise, so I didn't leave him waiting.

"He isn't the one for me. There was nothing real between us."

"You're not going to elaborate more? He just wasn't the 'one'?" He made air quotes.

"What else is there to say? There were no sparks, all he ever wanted to talk about was our future careers and how great it was that our families would join if we got married."

"Is that all he talked about? Last time I checked, eighteen-year-old boys had other things on their minds."

"Dad!" I snapped. There are certain conversations a girl never wants to have with her father.

Evidently he got the hint. "All right, I'll drop it, but who would have believed a daughter of your mother and I would grow up to be a romantic."

"Did you ever think I ended up this way *because* of your relationship with Mom?" I could go on for hours about everything that was wrong in the relationship between my parents, but the cliff notes are that they were married five years and split up two years after I was born.

As though he could read my thoughts, Dad looked at me sympathetically. "I don't mean to disillusion you sweetie, but fairytale endings don't happen in the real world. I'm not going to sit here and tell you that you should date Toby, but I want you to understand that if you spend your whole life searching for perfection you are going to be alone, miserable, and old."

"Wow. You are such an optimist, Dad." I tried to shake his words off, but I couldn't quite get the image of myself as an old cat lady out of my head.

"You know it." He signaled for the waiter. "Let's go ahead and order."

After that, lunch was pleasant enough. The food came quickly and was a nice change from the fast food we ate on the road. We discussed our jobs for the summer. Dad was making us work at the front desk, convinced it would give me real insight into the hotel business.

"What do you ladies have planned for tonight?" he asked as he signaled for the check.

"I'm not sure, maybe we'll head out to explore a bit," I said vaguely.

"Have a good time, but be smart. Things can get pretty wild down here."

"Like you have to worry about us getting into trouble Mr. Davis," Jess said sweetly.

"It's not you girls I'm worried about. You are walking targets for men to take advantage of. Stay together and be alert."

"Next you are going to be giving us a curfew."

"Yes, because it's so crazy for a father to worry about his eighteen-year-old-daughter out in the French Quarter." He shook his head. "I trust you, so I'll stop the lecture, but one thing."

"Yes?"

"My room is right down the hall from yours."

"Duly noted." I kissed his cheek before Jess and I headed back upstairs to our room.

Three

"You're no fun!" Jess cried out as I untangled her from the latest guy she was hanging on. It only took a few drinks for Jess to get tipsy. Maybe it would have taken longer if she didn't insist on accepting every drink a guy offered us, and there were lots. I played along at first, but it didn't take long for me to switch to club soda. Someone needed to stay sober.

"I'm fun. I'm so much fun that I want to dance." Grabbing Jess's hand, I pulled her into the center of the bar. The thick layer of smoke permeating the air seemed to highlight the intense lighting.

"But I was having fun with Drew!" she whined, swaying drunkenly to the music as we danced with little space between us. We were attracting attention, but I pretended not to notice.

"His name is Dave, by the way." I laughed.

"Drew, Dave, same thing."

"I distinctly remember you agreeing to a girl's night out. No guys, remember?"

Jess sighed dramatically. "Fine. Besides it's probably almost our turn."

"You don't actually expect me to sing karaoke in front of everyone do you?"

"Of course I do. If I'm staying away from boys then you're singing karaoke," she said, almost yelling to be heard over the loud music.

16

When Jess asked Billy the bellboy where we should go if we wanted to really do Bourbon Street for our first night, he suggested the Cat's Meow. As soon as Jess found out it was a karaoke bar she ran over to sign us up. I hadn't actually expected us to stay long enough to get to our turn, and I was starting to regret cutting myself off from the alcohol. Singing karaoke sober sounded horrendous.

"I need a drink."

She laughed. "It's usually me who says that."

We were halfway to the bar when I heard our names called. I froze. It looked like I was singing sober.

This time it was Jess's turn to tug me along.

The first bars of *Girls Just Want to Have Fun* started right as we reached the stage. Jess began to belt it out, and reluctantly I joined in. I reassured myself that everyone in the bar was intoxicated, and I didn't know any of them. By the second verse I started getting into it. There are plenty of things I'm good at but singing isn't one of them. I knew the screaming and catcalls that filled the bar had nothing to do with our voices, but I decided to go with it. Running a hand through my hair, I moved my hips to the music and went all out. It actually felt pretty good once I forgot about the audience and just let go.

Met with applause, we made exaggerated curtseys before stepping down as the music faded out. Any adrenaline I felt during the song quickly disappeared.

"AHH! I love New Orleans!" Jess screamed as we headed away from the stage.

I smiled to myself, not willing to admit out loud that I kind of enjoyed it too.

"You look like you could use this." I was startled by a seductively smooth voice, as I felt something cold pushed into my palm.

I glanced up. Intense gray-blue eyes stared back at me, as I recognized the guy from the hotel. Surprised to see him again, I merely nodded before bringing the shot to my lips.

"What was that?" I spat out while the liquor continued to burn my throat.

"A jaeger shot." He laughed lightly. "Feeling better?"

"Yeah. I can't believe I did that." I peered over my shoulder at the stage where another group was starting their rendition of *Time of my Life*.

"It really wasn't so bad. It was more entertaining than if Cyndi Lauper performed it herself." Raking his eyes from my toes back up to my face, he spent an annoying amount of time studying my legs. Long legs were nice, but not when they attracted the wrong type of attention. Normally I would call a guy on mentally undressing me, but I was too busy taking my own inventory. Finished, I glanced around for Jess but couldn't see her in the crowd.

"So, thanks for the shot, but I need to find my friend."

"Hey, you can't run off on me again." He didn't say it like a question, more like a demand and it annoyed me. "Besides, your friend appears to be unavailable."

I followed his gaze and noticed Jess flirting with Dave again. "Run off on you again? That implies we have run into each other before." I tried for coy; I wasn't going to let this guy unnerve me. Sure, he had the most amazing set of eyes I had ever seen, but I wasn't interested.

"I saw you at the Crescent City Hotel this afternoon, but you took off before I could say hello." He leaned in closer to me, trying to be heard over the loud music.

"Oh, I didn't notice you."

He smiled, ignoring my comment. "You here for vacation?"

"I'm here for work actually, at the hotel."

"Are you around for the whole summer then?"

I allowed myself to really look at him. My earlier estimate of his height was dead on; he was much taller than my 5 feet 9 inches.

I finally answered. "Yeah, I'm here until I start school in the fall."

"All right, so where are you going to school?"

"Princeton." I braced myself for his response.

"Nice," he said in a way that suggested he wasn't impressed.

"You in school?"

"Yeah, I'm going to be a senior at Tulane."

"Oh, so you live here?"

"Born and raised," he said proudly.

"I didn't think locals hung out at places like this."

"We don't usually, but they're great spots to meet girls from out of town."

I shook my head. "Ah, so you're one of them."

"One of who?"

"The type to prey on innocent tourists."

"Innocent tourists? You make me sound like the big bad wolf."

"And you're not?" I questioned.

"Only if you're Red Riding Hood," he said flirtatiously.

"Wow, that's original." I caught myself staring at his eyes again and decided it was time to end the conversation. "Well, nice talking to you."

"Hey, I didn't even get your name yet."

"Allie."

"Is that short for Allison?"

"Yes, but no one calls me Allison." I cursed myself. Why couldn't I just walk away from this guy? I briefly regretted my decision to swear off men because if I hadn't this one would be exactly my type: tall, strong, and confident. He was exactly the kind to avoid.

"I'm Levi," he said, holding out his hand.

"Is that short for something?"

I accepted his handshake and he held it a moment longer than necessary. "Leviathan. But you can call me whatever you like," he said suggestively.

"Well, nice to meet you." I started to walk away and ran right into Jess.

"Wow, it's hotel bar guy," she said way too loudly. She was evidently drunker than I realized.

"So you did notice me," Levi said almost in a whisper, so close to my ear that I could feel his breath on my neck. I said nothing, not willing to give his ego anymore ammo. I couldn't help but notice how good he smelled, but not like cologne, it was probably his aftershave.

"So, does that mean you changed your mind?" Jess leaned into me drunkenly.

"Changed her mind? About what?" Levi asked looking at me questioningly. I silently prayed that for the first time ever Jess could keep her mouth shut.

"Allie's sworn off men, or so she claims," Jess said, taking a long drink from a beer.

"Is that so?" Levi asked with a glimmer of humor in his eyes.

"Yes, not that it's any of your business."

"Any particular reason why?"

"None that I wish to explain."

"She thinks it's because she has bad luck with relationships, but really it's because no one is good enough for her," Jess said all in one breath.

Ouch. I knew Jess could be a mean drunk, but this was harsh even for her.

I was angry and in no mood to continue hanging out with Levi, but Jess was way too out of it to leave her by herself. I took the next best option. "I think I need another drink."

"My pleasure," Levi said quickly, "What can I get you?"

"Surprise me."

"I will." He winked. "I'm good at surprises."

Once Levi was fixated on getting the bartender's attention, I grabbed Jess's arm. "What the hell is wrong with you?"

"What do you mean? I'm just being honest."

"No, you're being obnoxious."

"You would only care if you liked him. Do you?" she pressed.

"It doesn't matter."

Levi returned holding two drinks and gestured with his arm toward a table in the corner where two guys were seated. "A few of my friends are sitting over there, care to join us?"

Jess shrugged. "Why not?"

Levi looked at me and I nodded, too annoyed at the situation to care.

The two guys stopped their conversation as we reached the table. Both were as broad as Levi, one had black hair and the other was blond.

"Girls, this is Jared and Owen." He gestured to the two. "And this is Allie and Jess."

"Well, hello there," Jared said with a grin as he looked us over.

The blond, Owen, nodded. "Hey."

Jess sat down next to Jared who lost no time turning to talk to her. Levi put our drinks down in front of two empty chairs, and he pulled out the one closest to the wall for me. I took the seat, grateful that it was far away from Jess. I was starting to second-guess my decision to invite her down.

Levi took a swig from his drink. "You can't really mean to punish the entire male gender for the errors of a few." I picked up my own and sipped it slowly, completely unsure of what I was drinking, but enjoying the sweet distraction.

"Because it would be really unfair to do that," Levi said playfully.

"Um, can we please talk about something else?" I turned away, but thanks to my seat next to the wall the only other place to look was straight ahead at Owen. He watched us with an amused expression.

"Sure, for now. What made you decide to take the job at the hotel?" he asked, pulling my attention away from Owen.

"Oh, I needed a job and my dad was able to get it for me."

"Because Allie's dad is super rich and bought the place," Jess butted in. I didn't even realize she was listening to us. I shot her a dirty look. I may not have wanted to get involved with Levi, but I

23

didn't want him thinking I was a spoiled rich girl. I was tired of getting thrown in with the stereotype.

"What? It's true."

"Your dad bought the Crescent City Hotel?" Jared asked, really looking at me for the first time.

"Yeah. The deal went through earlier this year." I picked up my drink again and downed it.

"I guess you liked it?" Levi asked as I replaced my empty cup.

"Maybe a little. What was it?"

"Want another?" Levi asked without answering the question.

"No, don't worry about it; I can get one for myself if you'll tell me what it is." I didn't want Levi to think I was indebted to him for buying me drinks.

"I'm getting up anyway," he said as he stood. I grumbled. "Besides, if you don't know what it is you will have to let me keep buying them for you." He grinned before walking away.

"You want anything?" Jared asked Jess.

"Definitely, but I'll come with you, I want some shots." Jess and Jared walked off leaving me alone at the table with Owen.

"Wow, there is a first time for everything," Owen said, breaking the silence.

"Hmm?"

"Usually Levi has girls eating out of his hand by now but you keep trying to blow him off."

"Yeah, I'm not interested."

Owen laughed. "I don't think that Levi understands uninterested."

"Well, then this can be a learning experience for him."

"Something tells me this is going to be fun to watch." He grinned.

We sat awkwardly for a moment before Levi returned with the drinks. I felt a tiny twinge of guilt accepting another drink from him when I wasn't interested in getting involved with him, but he had already bought it so I decided to drink it anyway.

"It looked like you two were having a good conversation, did I miss anything?" Levi asked.

"Nothing worth repeating," I said quickly.

Owen smiled. "Well, Allie was telling me that she isn't interested in you."

Damn, could no one keep their mouth shut? I figured the fact that I didn't give him my number at the end of the night would have been straightforward enough.

Levi leaned in closer to me but spoke to Owen. "It's because she's sworn off men. But I think I'll just have to be the exception."

By this point, I had already had quite a few sips of my new drink. The combination of the late night and alcohol made me a little tipsy. "What in the world would make you think that you would be an exception?"

"One, you're attracted to me and two, I can be very persistent."

"I am not attracted to you!" I said rather loudly right as Jess and Jared arrived back at the table.

"Like hell you're not," Jess said before bursting into laughter. Jared looked from Jess, to me, to Levi.

"You know there could be a few females alive that are not into you Levi," Jared mocked.

"It's always a possibility, but that's not the case this time. She likes me, she just won't admit it." Levi scooted his seat closer to me, effectively pinning me against the wall. Between my buzz and the heat of his body, I was starting to get a little dizzy.

I sighed and closed my eyes. As angry as I was at Jess, I couldn't leave her alone with these guys. I had to wait her out. My eyes were still closed when I felt Levi's arm move around my shoulder. "Relax."

I opened my eyes and his face was right next to mine. I tried to look away but he wouldn't let me break the gaze. With a hand under my chin, he forced me to look up at him.

"Stop looking away. I love green eyes."

"Does that line usually work for you?" I ribbed.

"Usually. I'm guessing it's not going to work tonight."

"Not a chance."

"I'll just have to get more creative."

"You do that."

"So, what do you think of New Orleans so far?" Owen asked.

Jess answered. "It's been fantastic. It's so awesome to get away and meet new people." She ran a hand down Jared's arm, letting him know who she was excited to have met.

"And what about you, Allie?" Levi's lips curled up into a small smile.

"Well, considering we've been here less than twenty-four hours, it's hard to have much of an impression, but I like it so far."

"You'll have to keep me posted as you have more time to form an opinion."

"I'll be sure to keep you updated." I rolled my eyes.

"You girls want to see the rest of the Quarter?" Jared asked.

"Yes!" Jess answered immediately. "We haven't seen anything but here and the hotel."

"You interested?" Levi whispered into my ear again. The tone of his voice and the proximity of his lips to my ear made me wonder what he was really asking.

"Sure. Why not?" I took one last drink, straightened my skirt and stood up.

Levi put his arm around me as we headed toward the door. "I guarantee you're going to love New Orleans."

Maneuvering away from him, I answered absently. "Is that right?" My attention was diverted to watching Jess and Jared grope each other. I stifled a groan.

If the sight of people drinking out in the open wasn't enough of a hint that I was far from home, the fact that it was still hot at 11:00 p.m. made it impossible to deny. Walking through the crowded streets, feeling the sticky heat on my neck, I was happy to be in a skirt.

After walking down St. Peter's Street, we ended up in Jackson Square. Surrounded by wrought iron railings, the square was full of activity. Everywhere I looked musicians performed and artists had their work displayed.

"Care to have your fortune read?" a palm reader called out as we passed.

"No thanks." I waved her off.

"Are you sure you don't want a glimpse into your future?"

"I prefer surprises."

"Same here," Jess agreed as we continued walking. "This is too cool. It might be even better than Washington Square Park," she said in awe and looking around. Like most New Yorkers, there was only one city for us.

"Of course this is just where all the tourists hang out. There are much cooler places, hon. Maybe I'll show you sometime," Jared crooned.

"Like where, your apartment?" I raised an eyebrow. Jared seemed like a textbook player. I hoped Jess knew what she was dealing with.

"Why, you want to see my place?" he challenged me without removing his arm from around Jess.

If he expected to unnerve me, he had another thing coming. "In your dreams."

I heard Levi's deep laugh from behind me as he wrapped his arms around my waist. "Would you change your mind about that if you knew I was his roommate?"

"Why would that change my mind?" I spun out of his embrace and turned my attention to a couple playing guitars. I listened for a few minutes, pulling a dollar from my purse to throw into the hat in front of them. Looking up after leaving the money, I startled as I noticed a black crow staring intently at me from the fence behind the musicians. "Creepy."

"What's creepy?" Owen came up beside me.

"That crow."

"You're not a big fan of birds, I take it?" he asked with the hint of a smile.

"I like birds fine, but when a black crow sits there staring at me it weirds me out. It looks like it might attack or something."

"It's not going to attack, it's just watching."

"Okay, well, it's still creepy."

Owen laughed. "I heard you say you didn't want to stay out too late. I thought I'd warn you that if

29

you want a chance of getting your friend home tonight you should probably speak up."

I followed Owen's gaze to where Jess and Jared were making out. "Thanks for the heads up."

"The heads up on what?" For the second time that night Levi interrupted a conversation with Owen.

"I was simply suggesting she pry Jess away from Jared if she wants to get her home tonight."

"What's the hurry? The night is young." Levi shot me a devilish smile.

"We have our first day of work tomorrow," I explained.

"Your first day of work at your father's hotel. Can't you skip out?"

"No! I am not missing my first day of work. I'm not like that."

"Really? Maybe I can learn more about you tomorrow night? Maybe over dinner?" Levi asked.

"Not a chance."

"Oh, that's right; you think you've sworn off men."

Rolling my eyes, I didn't bother to respond. "Jess, let's go!"

"Now? Seriously?" Jess whined.

"I'm sure you can meet up with your friend another time." I didn't want to ruin Jess's fun, but things were getting intense between her and Jared, and I didn't know how much of a role alcohol was playing.

"What's the rush all of a sudden?" Jared asked, giving me the evil eye.

"Owen decided to point out the late hour to her," Levi said emotionlessly.

"What the hell, man?" Jared lunged at Owen; his eyes looked like they had turned solid black. I shook my head as I watched Levi put himself between his friends. I must have had more to drink than I thought.

"Let it go, Jared. I'm sure we'll have plenty of opportunities to see them again. We'll walk you girls home." Levi wasn't asking and I didn't protest, figuring it couldn't hurt to let them walk us.

By the time we reached the hotel, Jess's buzz had started wearing off, and she looked ready to collapse on the spot. I watched her say good bye to Jared while I waved at Levi and Owen. "Goodnight."

"Nice to meet you." Owen smiled.

"I'll be seeing you," Levi said before turning to walk away.

I barely had enough energy to brush my teeth and wash my makeup off before heading to bed. I knew it was going to be a crazy summer.

Four

"Which one of you is Mr. Davis's daughter?" A woman in a tailored suit approached Jess and I as we waited in the lobby.

"You must be Natalie." I shook the blonde woman's hand politely. "I'm Allie and this is Jess."

She smiled warmly. "Pleasure to meet you both." Striking and even taller than me, Natalie wasn't exactly what I expected the manager of the hotel to look like. I don't know what I expected, maybe a middle-aged man or something. Then again, my dad said he did the hiring himself, and he certainly had a weakness for attractive women.

"Same to you. We're really looking forward to working at the hotel this summer." I nudged Jess.

"We're super excited!" Jess's fake enthusiasm didn't seem to register with Natalie.

"Mr. Davis made it clear that you are only required to work set daytime shift hours, but if either of you are serious about working in the hotel industry, you should consider working some evening shifts to get a better understanding of the 24-hour nature of the business."

Deciding to keep my thoughts about how little interest we had in the industry to myself, I settled for a simple answer. "I understand, but for now I think we'll stick with days."

Natalie led us over to the front desk and introduced us to the desk clerk on duty. Probably in her late thirties, Adie seemed pleasant enough.

"It's nice to meet you girls. I'm looking forward to getting some more time off this summer. With my kids home from school, I could use it."

"It's nice to meet you too." I shook Adie's hand and Jess followed my lead.

Natalie excused herself. "Adie should be able to show you everything you need to know, but if you have any questions or need anything I'll be in my office."

I smiled. "Thanks, I'm sure we'll be fine."

The morning dragged. Although not hung over, I wasn't feeling like myself. I had slept fitfully with dreams that slipped away before I woke up. Adie showed us how to work the computers, and she explained that unless someone was checking in or out, we could usually direct most questions to the concierge if one was working.

Adie left around noon, leaving Jess and I to our own devices.

"Hey girls," Billy said when he came by the desk.

"Hi Billy!" Jess turned to give him her undivided attention.

"I'm going to take a break for lunch; do you guys want to join me?" He leaned casually against the desk.

"Sure," Jess said eagerly.

"You can go, but Adie just left and we can't leave the desk empty so I'll stay here," I explained.

"Oh, then forget it."

"Go ahead, I don't mind."

"You sure?" Jess tried to act like she didn't care, but her face pleaded with me. So much for being into Jared, she certainly seemed excited to see Billy.

"Yeah, go ahead," I repeated.

"Okay, great. I'll be back soon so you can get something next."

"All right, have fun."

I played around on my phone for a while, downloading some apps I didn't actually need. A few guests came to check in, but thankfully, I was able to direct most questions to the concierge. I was feeling all right, but I needed caffeine. I noticed a sandy haired guy working at the bar and decided to go over to get a Diet Coke.

"Hi there. Are you Allie or Jess?" the bartender asked as soon as I walked over.

"Hi… How did you know our names?" I said slowly.

He laughed. "Well, how many new employees do you think started today?"

"Oh, that makes sense. I'm Allie."

"Alex. Pleasure to meet you." He shook my hand.

"Same."

"So you're the boss's daughter, huh? What can I get you? Not going to drink on the job your first day, are you?"

I tried to ignore the boss's daughter comment even though it irked me. "No, I'm not that desperate. I could use a Diet Coke though."

"Coming right up." He smiled as he popped open a can of soda and handed it to me.

I took a sip, and started to take a seat when Jess's voice rang through the lobby.

"Oh my god Allie, I'm so sorry we were gone so long!" She joined me at the bar, Billy next to her.

"This must be Jess?" Alex asked with the hint of a smile.

"Oh no, what did Allie say about me?"

"Nothing, we've only been talking a minute," Alex explained.

Billy exchanged glances with Alex. "Well, I'm glad you guys met. I thought we could all go out after work. Jess claims she wants to try some southern food."

"Southern food, eh?" Alex arched an eyebrow.

"I want my experience down here to be authentic."

"Oh yeah?" Alex laughed. "You in, Allie?"

"Sure, but I should probably get some lunch now."

"I'm sorry again for taking so long, but here's a peace offering." Jess pulled a plastic bag from behind her. I took it, and peeked inside to find a sandwich.

"Peace offering accepted. Let's get back to work."

***

After running upstairs to our rooms to change, we headed down to the lobby to meet Billy and Alex.

As the elevator doors opened, I noticed the infuriatingly familiar outline of Levi walking toward us. Thankfully, he was looking the other way. Jess had already started getting out, so I yanked her back inside, letting the doors close again.

"What the hell was that?" she asked, rubbing her arm where I grabbed her.

"Sorry, I'm just not in the mood to deal with him right now."

"Fine. I guess it's better this way. It would have been awkward to have tried to talk to both Jared and Billy at the same time."

I shook my head.

By the time the doors opened again, Levi and his friends had already moved over to the bar where a female bartender now worked.

Alex and Billy were waiting for us by the front entrance.

"You know those guys?" Alex asked, noticing the direction of my attention.

"We hung out with them last night," Jess said nonchalantly.

Alex stopped to look at us as we walked out into the still bright sun. "You should really stay away from them. They aren't the kind of people you kids should be hanging out with."

36

"Kids?" I asked as we walked. "As compared to you and your advanced years?"

"I'm twenty-four. You just graduated from high school, right?"

"Yeah, so?"

"Well then, you're a kid. Trust me; the next few years will make a big difference."

"Okay, whatever. I don't plan to spend more time with them, but now I'm curious. Why warn us about them?" I asked as we walked down the street toward the restaurant. Alex had apparently not heard my question or decided not to answer it.

A few minutes later we arrived at Café Maspero. Even on a weekday night, a line had formed outside. Billy assured us that this was a mainstay French Quarter restaurant, and we had to try it at least once.

Eventually we were seated at a table in the middle of the bustling restaurant and we all ordered some sodas.

"Where are you girls from?" Alex asked.

"New York," I answered.

"The city?"

"No, the suburbs."

Alex got excited. "What part? I'm from Connecticut."

"Really? We're from Westchester." I was surprised to find another northeasterner. "What brought you down here?"

"I came down for school and never left. This city has a funny way of doing that to you. It gets under your skin."

"Even more than New York?" Jess asked. "I can't imagine loving a city more than that."

Alex smiled faintly. "I thought that too, but there is just something about New Orleans that's addicting. I can't really explain it."

I noticed Billy was quiet and tried to pull him back into the conversation. "Where are you from?"

"Shreveport. I'm a Louisiana boy through and through." He grinned.

"Cool."

As the conversation hit a lull, I decided to push Alex again on his comment about Levi and his friends. I had no intention of spending more time with Levi, but I knew Jess wanted to see Jared again.

"You never answered my question. Why should we stay away from them?"

"Away from who?" Billy interjected.

"Those jacked up guys who are always at the hotel," Alex supplied.

"Oh, them." Billy gave a disgusted look. "Yeah, Alex is right, stay away."

"But why?" I was getting tired of the elusive answers.

"How much did your father tell you about the hotel? Did he tell you anything about who he bought it from?" Alex asked.

"He told me nothing. For someone who wants me to take over his business he never bothers to give me any information."

Alex looked like he was contemplating how much to reveal. "There's just something off about them."

"Could you possibly be less vague?" I didn't bother to hide my impatience.

Billy gave a frustrated sigh. "Fine, it's like this. You know how there are no basements in New Orleans?"

"I didn't, but okay. What does that have to do with those guys?"

"There are no basements because we're below sea level." He waited for us to acknowledge that we understood. "For some reason, there is still a button for the basement in the elevator at the hotel. But if you hit the button nothing happens, okay?"

"And?" Jess pressed.

"Those guys are always hanging out at the hotel. I've watched them. Whenever they get on the elevator the button for the basement lights up as though they are actually getting off there. It makes no sense," Billy explained.

"So first you say there is no basement, and now they're getting off there?" Jess rolled her eyes.

"I know. It makes no sense. Either they are going to another floor and making the elevator look like it's going down to the basement, or they

39

are doing something weird underneath the building," Billy continued.

"Whoa, do you realize how crazy you sound? Besides, what are you doing staring at the elevator numbers when they get on?" I asked.

"I'm a bellhop. I'm supposed to hang out by the elevators."

"Plus, they are always with some pretty shady characters. And I mean shady for New Orleans, which says a lot," Alex added.

I wasn't sure what he meant by that exactly, but I went with it. "All right, so we should stay away from them because they keep weird company and get off on the nonexistent basement level of the hotel. Got it."

Even though Billy and Alex seemed a bit out there on the topic, it still gnawed at me. I would have to ask my dad about the basement. If there was a way down there, he would have access.

Jess played with a piece of hair that had fallen loose from her ponytail. "They're actually pretty cool guys, so you don't have to worry. Anyway what are you going to order, Allie?"

"I'm not sure, maybe the chef salad or something," I said absently, scanning the menu.

"No way. We came here so you two can try some New Orleans food, and that's what we're going to do." Billy smiled.

"What do you suggest?"

"Let me order," Alex offered.

I looked at Jess. "Should we trust him?"

"Might as well."

When the waiter returned, Alex and Billy ordered enough food to feed ten. I hadn't heard of some of the dishes, but I'm usually an adventurous eater so I didn't mind.

An hour later, I was so stuffed I could hardly move. I loved how flavorful everything was, and even liked the greasiness of it all. "All right, so the jambalaya is incredible and let's be honest, what doesn't taste good fried?"

"Next time we'll have to get you hushpuppies," Billy said.

"Hushpuppies? Aren't those shoes or something?" I asked confused.

Alex and Billy burst out laughing.

"What?"

"A hushpuppy is like fried cornbread."

"Oh, wow, you learn something new every day."

Five

"Remind me again why I agreed to this?" I asked as Jess and I finished getting ready in front of the mirror in the bathroom.

"Because you're my best friend and Jared is hot. Oh and whether you admit it or not you want Levi."

"Don't push your luck."

"It's going to be fun. We've been here two weeks and still haven't left the Quarter," Jess pouted.

"True. It'll be nice to see more of the city, but does it really have to be with them?"

"I don't know why you care. If you aren't into Levi then what are you afraid is going to happen?"

"Nothing," I said quickly. "Are you ready?"

"Definitely. You look awesome."

"Thanks." It didn't take long to discover that lightweight sundresses were the best wardrobe choice for the climate. Wearing a pink halter dress, I slipped into a pair of black flip-flops as we headed out the door.

Levi, Jared, and Owen were waiting for us when we got off the elevator.

"Hey there Allison." Levi blatantly checked me out. He didn't look too bad himself, dressed once again in a fitted Lacoste shirt and dark jeans.

"It's Allie."

"Oh yeah, I forgot."

"I'm sure."

"Are you girls ready to see uptown?" Owen asked.

"Sure, should we follow you, or get an address for my GPS?"

"Neither." Levi ushered us towards the door. "We're taking the streetcar. That way you don't have to worry about a designated driver."

"Will it still be running when we need to get home?" I asked.

"This is New Orleans, it runs all night," Jared said. I could practically hear him rolling his eyes.

We walked two blocks to the corner of Canal and St. Charles and hopped on the streetcar just as it got ready to pull away. Levi pushed my money aside as I tried to figure out how to insert it into the machine. "I've got this."

As I prepared to argue, the car jerked forward, propelling me backwards into Levi's arms. "Easy does it, darling."

Carefully walking down the aisle, I slid into an empty seat and of course, Levi slipped in next to me.

"So where are we going exactly?" I asked after glancing across the aisle to see Jess unabashedly flirting with Jared.

"The Maple Leaf. It's a bar that always has great live music. You're going to like it."

"Glad to know you are now an expert on what I like."

"I'm an expert on a lot of things."

Levi's thigh brushed against mine as he stretched out his legs, and I couldn't ignore the way it affected me. Leaning against the side of the car, I moved as far away from him as possible. With the windows open, the breeze cooled me off as we continued uptown. I watched the city go by, all too aware of Levi's proximity. As hard as I tried to fight it, there was no denying my attraction to him, and I had a feeling he knew it.

"Beautiful, aren't they?"

I felt goosebumps from where Levi's breath tickled my skin. His closeness was killing me. "The homes? Yeah, they're gorgeous. Is this the Garden district?"

"Yes. Home sweet home."

"Have you always lived here?" I asked.

"Born and raised, and I never want to move anywhere else."

"Really?" My interest was piqued enough that I turned toward him. His face was only inches from mine.

"Does that really surprise you?"

"I mean you told me you were from here, but don't most people our age want to explore new places?"

"Why explore when you have everything you need right here?" His intense gaze implied he was talking about me rather than the city.

"Yeah. Whatever." If he thought his corny lines were going to work on me, he was going to be sorely disappointed.

I looked back outside, watching the beautiful large homes lining the street while trying to ignore the electricity that clearly ran between us.

A half-hour later, I turned toward Levi when I felt his hand on my leg. "This is us." He pulled the cord to request a stop and we jumped off. "It's only a few blocks from here."

"Have a nice ride?" Jess asked, grabbing my hand.

"Splendid."

"It looked like you were enjoying yourself." Her impish grin matched her tone of voice.

I heard Levi laugh but ignored it.

"Yeah, I wouldn't have thought you noticed. You looked pretty distracted yourself."

"Unlike you, I'm not going to pretend otherwise." Jess picked up the pace, virtually skipping as she towed me along behind the guys.

With neon signs advertising beers I'd never heard of, the Maple Leaf was located in an unassuming two story building. Loud music hit me as soon as we walked into the bar. Still holding Jess's hand, we followed the guys through the crowd onto the patio out back.

45

"Owen!" a gorgeous redhead yelled out as she wrapped her arms around him in a hug.

Unraveling himself from her embrace Owen snapped at her. "Aww, damn it Hailey. I should have known you would be here."

"Don't bother hiding it, Owen; you know you're glad to see your favorite sister." She grinned.

"You mean my only sister."

Hailey ignored Owen's last comment, holding out her hand to shake ours. "Hi, I don't think we've met."

It took me a moment to process that her focus was on us. "I'm Allie."

"Jess."

"Nice to meet you. So you're friends with my brother then?"

"Sort of…"

"Enough of the twenty questions. We met them down at the hotel. Allie's dad owns the place now," Owen explained.

"Oh!" I watched as Hailey tried to compose her face into a smile but the look of shock was undeniable.

"Watch it, Hailey," Jared warned.

I opened my mouth to ask what the heck Hailey's reaction was about, but she didn't give me the chance. "It's really nice to meet you both. My best friends deserted me to spend the summer abroad, and I could really use some other girls around."

"Wait, Beth and Jill both left already? Who are you here with?" Owen asked. It was funny watching him go all big brother protector on her.

"I came by myself to meet up with Jamie. Not a big deal."

"Oh, okay, but don't leave by yourself."

"Like I can't take care of myself?" she said incredulously.

"Just humor me, Hailey."

"Sure." Hailey rolled her eyes. "God, older brothers can be annoying. Do you have any siblings, Allie?"

"Nope, I'm an only child."

"So lucky." Jess broke in. "I have four younger brothers and sisters."

"Four? Wow," Hailey said with surprise.

"Yeah, I know. Thankfully, I was always able to escape the chaos by crashing at Allie's because her mom is cool. She's so lucky."

"My mom is pretty cool," I admitted. Mom more than made up for Dad's absence. It's part of why I knew I had to go to Princeton. My mom went there too and she wanted us to have the shared experience. "And my house is quiet. But I wouldn't have minded a sibling."

"We all want what we don't have, am I right?" Hailey asked.

"Exactly."

"Are you girls done gossiping yet?" Jared whined, putting an arm around Jess.

"Gossiping? Yeah, okay." Hailey rolled her eyes again and this time I laughed.

"I got your drink for you," Levi said from behind and I realized I hadn't even noticed him leave. He held a glass towards me in one hand, while holding an Abita beer in his other.

I accepted the glass. "My drink?"

"You seemed to like it the other night."

"And you still aren't going to tell me what's in it?"

"Nope."

"Well, there are other ways of figuring it out."

"Are there now?" He arched an eyebrow.

"Uh-huh."

"You care to share?"

"Not right now." I smiled and took a seat at a table next to Owen. Before Levi could sit down next to me, Hailey jumped into the seat. The dirty look Levi gave Hailey wasn't lost on me.

There were a few other guys sitting at the table that started laughing when we sat down. I couldn't tell if it was about Hailey annoying Levi or the fact that Jess was sitting in Jared's lap. All the seats were taken.

I waited, curious as to how Levi was going to react.

"You can have my chair." One of the other guys at the table stood up quickly.

"That won't be necessary. I'm sure Allie and I can share."

Taken aback by how the guy was so willing to defer to Levi, I almost missed what Levi was suggesting. "You wish."

"Why? You afraid you might actually like it?" Levi said arrogantly. Almost everyone at the table laughed, even Jess, which annoyed me. Only Hailey stayed quiet.

His words sent chills down me because a part of me knew he was right. "Not a chance."

The laughter stopped, and I got the distinct impression that people didn't usually argue with Levi.

The whole situation seemed so dumb that I got up and walked inside. I watched the band play, drawn in immediately. I had never heard anything quite like it before. The band was comprised of a tuba, trombone, trumpet, and drummer. The music had a jazzy feel with a funky beat. Without meaning to, I started moving to the beat; this was not the kind of music that let you stay still. I finished my drink before placing it on the bar.

"I told you you'd like it here." Levi leaned on the bar next to me.

"I admit it's pretty cool. Who is this, by the way?"

"Oh, it's the Rebirth Brass Band. Heard of them?"

"I don't think so, but that isn't surprising. I'm not exactly up on the New Orleans music scene. Anyway, what was that all about back there?"

"What do you mean?"

"Why do people act like you walk on water or something?"

"How do you know I don't?" Levi handed me another drink, and I sipped it slowly this time. I needed to avoid getting drunk, my willpower around Levi was weak enough sober.

"Don't what?"

"Walk on water."

"Wow, you are even cockier than I thought."

Levi laughed and I hated how sexy it sounded.

"All right, I can't walk on water, but I can do other things very, very well."

"Oh yeah?" I sounded flirtier than I wanted to. The alcohol hit me harder than I expected, probably because I had skipped dinner.

"Let me show you."

The heated look in his eyes told me he was going to kiss me, and I didn't bother to stop him. Instead, I closed my eyes. His lips brushed mine lightly, and for a moment I thought that was it, but just as I prepared for him to pull away, his lips crushed mine more urgently.

The chaste kiss became much more as his strong arms went around me, pulling me against him. I reached up, twisting my hands in his hair.

His mouth tasted like a mixture of alcohol and sweetness, like a perfectly mixed cocktail.

He pulled his head back just enough to look at me but didn't move his hands. "Still going to pretend you aren't interested, Allison?"

Dazed, it took me a moment to answer. This only made Levi laugh which, of course, made me angry. "I told you to call me Allie."

"You said everyone calls you Allie. I'm not everyone."

"Are you always this frustrating?"

"Depends on who you ask."

Groaning, I placed my half-full glass on the bar and walked back outside. I didn't glance back, but Levi's laughter carried over the music and conversations, letting me know he was still right behind me.

Some seats had opened up at the table, so we avoided that drama the second time around. Of course, this time I would have had a harder time denying my interest in sitting on Levi's lap.

We hung out for hours, listening to the music pour into the courtyard from the bar. With Jess preoccupied with Jared, I got to spend a lot of time chatting with Hailey and we really hit it off. It turned out she had the same love of action movies that I did.

"Okay, so who would win in a fight, Jean-Claude Van Damme, Stephen Segal, Bruce Lee, or Jackie Chan?" Owen asked, after listening to Hailey and I dish on our favorite movies.

"Easy, Jean-Claude. I mean he's hot and bad ass. Can you get any better?" I answered immediately.

"Wait, so I'm not the only 18-year-old Jean-Claude fan? Nice!" Hailey gave me a high five.

"That's who you find hot?" Levi smirked. "But anyway, Owen, you left out Chuck Norris."

"Please no. Someone stop Levi from starting in on Chuck Norris. There are only so many of those jokes I can take." Hailey's hand hit the table hard, spilling some of our drinks, which for some reason seemed incredibly funny, so I started to laugh which only made her laugh too.

Thirty minutes later, we were no closer to reaching a consensus.

"Wow, is it really 2:30?" I squinted to look at the hands on my watch. I could barely keep my eyes open. I wished I had my glasses with me so I could take out my contacts. I settled for putting a few drops in my eyes. I was glad I'd remembered to throw them in my purse.

"Did you guys drive?" Hailey asked.

"No, we took the street car." Once I discovered how late it was all I wanted to do was go to sleep. I *so* didn't want to sit on a streetcar for a half hour.

"Why don't you guys come back to our place? It's really late anyhow," Jared suggested.

"That sounds like a great idea," Jess said quickly.

I fought back the urge to roll my eyes. "I'm sure it does, Jess."

"I'd have to agree." Levi smiled impishly.

"I'd invite you guys to crash at my house, but my parents will flip if they see that I've been drinking. I'm going to stay over at their place anyway," Hailey explained.

"You still live at home?"

"Yeah. I just graduated from high school."

"Oh, duh. You said you were eighteen." I thought about it for a minute before answering, weighing my options. "Okay, I'll stay at their place then." Somehow knowing Hailey was going to be there made it seem better. Besides, I was too exhausted to argue.

"I knew I'd be taking you home tonight," Levi whispered as we walked the few blocks to his place. I shrugged his arm off my shoulder instead of saying anything. He only laughed.

I barely noticed the outside of the house when we arrived, but I took notice of the inside. It's not like I had been in too many college boys' apartments before, but it wasn't what I expected. My image of dirty laundry and beer cans littering the floor was way off. The large living room was furnished with two black leather couches and a love seat. The only evidence that a bunch of guys lived there was the mess of video game controllers on the floor.

Giggling, Jess let Jared lead her to his room as soon as we arrived. I sat down on one of the couches.

"You are more than welcome to sleep in my bed." Levi slumped down next to me, putting his feet up on the circular ottoman that matched the couch.

"As tempting as that offer is, I'll take my chances out here." I slipped off my shoes and curled my legs up under me.

"Wow, Levi, you've never offered to let me take your bed before," Hailey said with exaggerated insult.

"And I'll never offer you my bed. If you don't want to sleep on the couch talk to your brother, or better yet, go home."

"Aww, you are always so sweet to me."

I laughed lightly at their banter. I liked how Hailey wasn't afraid to stick up for herself. No one else ever seemed to challenge Levi.

Owen joined us and we all talked for a while, mostly about all the trouble Levi, Owen, and Jared used to get into as kids. It turns out they all grew up together. I laughed more than I had in ages, and eventually I must have fallen asleep.

***

I was so comfortable when I woke up. Warm and more content than I had been in a while, I tried to stretch. I didn't have any room which was odd because my room at the hotel had a king size bed. I opened my eyes and first only saw the quilt; it was draped over me and someone else. I turned my body and looked right into those darn blue-gray eyes again.

54

"Good morning, beautiful."

"Oh god."

"Sleep well?"

I struggled to move, but he still had his arms around me. Relief flooded me as I discovered we were on a couch and not a bed.

"What are you doing here?"

"You're in my apartment, or did you forget?"

"I mean why are you sleeping on the couch with me? Why aren't you in your room?"

"Oh, I gave my bed to Hailey."

"But I thought you'd never…"

"I was just messing with her. Besides, I thought we could use the privacy."

"Was I really so zonked out I missed all of this?" I asked.

"You fell asleep in the middle of a conversation and were leaning against me. You looked too comfortable to disturb, so I just moved us a bit."

"I see. Well at least we're on the couch and not your bed." I was only pretending to be calm. I couldn't believe I had spent the night snuggled up with Levi. I was admittedly surprised, yet relieved he hadn't tried anything.

"Don't sound so relieved about it." His voice was playful but there was definitely a note of offense there.

"Hmm, yeah because it would have felt great to wake up in bed with a guy I don't know."

"You do know me, Allison."

"That again?" I asked him, still struggling to move out of his arms and off the couch.

"You are really cute when you get angry."

"Just shut up and let go of me so I can get the heck out of here."

"Wow, calm down. Aren't you going to let me make you breakfast? It's the least I can do for the girl I just spent the night with."

"I did not spend the night with you, we were on the couch." I blinked a few times, trying to get rid of the dryness in my eyes from sleeping in contacts.

"You spent the night in my arms, sweetheart. Sex or no sex, you can't argue that."

I groaned. Sudden laugher reminded me that we weren't really alone. I struggled against Levi again, and he finally relented so I could sit up. Owen walked into the room just as I stood up and made an attempt to get some wrinkles out of my dress. Levi remained lounging on the couch.

"Good morning. Did you enjoy the wonderful accommodations of our living room?"

"Where's Jess? Please tell me she's here somewhere," I said, not bothering to answer Owen. I was so over being made fun of.

"She's in with Jared," the guys both said at once.

"Um, could one of you please get her for me?" I asked, slipping my flip-flops back on and picking up my purse from the floor.

"There's no way I'm taking the chance of seeing Jared naked," Levi said sitting up and stretching.

"Gross. Fine, which room is his?"

"Seriously?"

"Yes, seriously. We have to be at work in like 20 minutes."

"Well, if you are already going to be late you might as well stay for breakfast."

"Which room is his?" I repeated.

Ten minutes later, I was walking out the front door with Jess trailing behind me. The cab was supposed to arrive any minute. "You could have at least let me get dressed!" Jess struggled to strap on her sandals.

"Thanks for an amazing night, Allison!" Levi laughed.

"I didn't tell you that you had to leave, just that I was leaving."

"Why are you so mad?"

"I *so* don't have to answer that."

"I thought you and Levi hit it off. You two were pretty cozy last night."

"Don't start. He has some nerve insinuating anything happened between us."

"Wait. So nothing happened?"

"No, thankfully I slept on the couch."

"Then why did Levi thank you for an amazing night?" Jess looked perplexed.

"He thinks he's a comedian and that falling asleep on the sofa counts as spending the night together."

Jess busted out laughing. "You two slept on the sofa together? Man, that guy must really be into you to forgo his own bed to curl up with you on the couch."

"Aren't I lucky?"

"I'd be jealous except that I had a great time with Jared last night." Jess smiled but something didn't look right about it, like it was forced.

"Please, no details," I begged.

I got through my morning work in one piece, but Jess didn't. She lasted maybe an hour before disappearing back upstairs to take a nap. I sat in the office behind the front desk doing mostly paperwork, drinking copious amounts of water, and trying to forget the night before. Obviously Jess was into Jared, so I was already trying to come up with excuses for why I wouldn't hang out with his friends, other than the obvious reason that I wanted to avoid Levi.

***

"Ready for lunch?" I looked up from the pile of papers in front of me with a start.

"What are you doing back here, Levi?"

"Oh, Natalie told me I could come back."

58

"Oh, did she?" I didn't want to get angry with the manager, but it annoyed me that she would just let him back into the office.

"Yeah. You ready?"

"I'm not having lunch with you." I tried to keep my voice down so none of the other employees would hear. Unfortunately, Levi didn't do the same.

"Well, you left without letting me make you breakfast this morning, so I thought I could at least take you to lunch." I felt the eyes of everyone in the office staring at me. I got up, grabbed Levi's arm and dragged him down the hall.

"I don't know what kind of game you're playing, but I'm not having it."

"What game? It's just lunch."

"So, you just like humiliating me in front of the people I work with?"

"That humiliated you?"

"Of course it did!" I said exasperated. "Now they think I slept with you."

"And that's a problem because…"

"Because this is my dad's hotel. Okay, Levi? My dad's. I don't need my dad hearing about this and thinking his daughter is some sort of slut."

"Being slutty would imply spending the night with lots of guys, not just one. Heck, you can even tell him I'm your boyfriend if it makes you feel better."

"My what?"

"Your boyfriend."

59

"Do you even know what that word means? Have you ever had a relationship that lasted more than a few days?" I had no idea what his dating history was, but he seemed like a player to me and I was angry.

"There is a first time for everything. Most girls would want to tame me."

"Tame you? Oh my god, leave. Just leave, okay?"

"Not until you agree to go out with me."

"You have to be kidding me."

"Not at all. I have no place to be, I'm staying here until you agree."

"Why? What angle are you playing?"

"First you accuse me of playing games and now angles. You aren't very trusting, Allison."

"It's Allie! And you haven't given me a reason to trust you!"

"Let me." I noticed a few employees peeking around the corner to see what was going on.

"Okay."

"Dinner tonight? I'd say lunch but I'd rather give you time to cool down."

"Don't you ever give up?"

"Never. I'm not leaving until you say yes."

I sighed. "Fine. Coffee Friday night. Then you leave me alone."

"I'll pick you up at 8:00 then."

"Sure, whatever. Now leave."

"I'll miss you too." He turned and walked away with a huge grin on his face.

Six

The week passed painfully slow. After a full day's work, I was more than happy to relax in our room, but it was strange that Jess suddenly seemed to not have any interest in going out. On Thursday morning, she didn't even get out of bed.

"You do realize we have work in ten minutes, right?" I asked, poking my head into her room.

"I'm just not feeling well. Is it okay if I skip today?"

"Sure. Feel better. Do you need anything before I go?"

"No. Don't worry," she assured me.

"Okay. See you later."

Jess didn't look particularly sick, but I figured playing hooky for one day wasn't a big deal. Still, something wasn't adding up, she just wasn't herself. I headed downstairs ready for a quiet morning of work. My quiet time didn't last long.

"What's up with Jess?" Billy asked. He had made a habit of hanging out at the desk with us whenever there was a lull in work for him—which was anytime but check in and check out. We saw a lot of each other.

"I have no clue. She refused to get up this morning. She's in a funk or something."

"Is she sick?" he asked worriedly.

"I don't think so."

"Have you tried to talk to her?" Adie joined in the conversation. She seemed really concerned.

"I tried, but she isn't saying anything. I honestly don't know what to do. She hasn't wanted to do anything and she's barely eating. I'm wondering if I should call her mom."

"If you are even questioning it you probably should," Adie advised. "A mother needs to know when her child is upset."

"Maybe I should try to talk to her one more time, and if there is no change I'll call?"

"That sounds reasonable," Adie agreed.

"Please let me know if I can do anything." Billy really was a nice guy and he cared about her. Too bad Jess never went for the nice guys. But if I was being honest I never did either.

***

In all of my years of knowing Jess, I had only seen her cry twice. The first time was when her beloved Golden Retriever died. The other was when her grandparents moved away. Walking into her room during my lunch break was number three.

"Hey, you all right?" I asked tentatively as I pushed open the door. "Wait, why are you packing?"

"I'm leaving. I'm sorry to run out on you, but I would rather spend the summer at home." Jess jammed clothes haphazardly into an open suitcase on her bed.

I felt a moment of panic. What the heck was going on? "Umm, okay. You going to expand on that at all?"

"I don't want to be here and besides Emmett texted me, I might try to work things out with him."

"Seriously? What happened to him being like a lost dog who can't get a clue when he's not wanted?" Jess had dumped her longtime boyfriend back in September because she wanted to have a fun senior year. He'd tried to get back together with her a few times, but she always refused.

"I changed my mind."

"What's really going on?"

She started sobbing. I sat down on the bed pulling her into my arms. "What happened? You have to tell me."

"I shouldn't have done it."

"Done what?"

"*It*. With Jared."

"Oh… Did he hurt you or something?" I asked, afraid of the answer.

"It was my first time," she mumbled and at first, I thought I'd heard her wrong.

"What did you say?"

"It was my first time. I was a virgin, okay."

I tried to rein in my surprise. Instead of asking why she had pretended to sleep with guys before, I asked the more immediate question. "Then why did you?"

"He didn't ask me if I was sure. Guys always ask if you're sure you want to… It's always my way out. Jared didn't ask."

"Oh, Jess." I hugged her again and let her tears soak through my shirt. Somehow, my "anything goes" friend had managed to get seriously hurt and I couldn't help but feel responsible. Jess was always so flippant about hooking up with guys that I hadn't worried about her after the first night. She seemed so interested in him I didn't see any reason to interfere. It wasn't an excuse and I felt like an incredibly self-absorbed and horrible friend.

"You won't hate me for leaving, will you?" Jess appeared so vulnerable with her tear-streaked face. It was such a contrast to her usual bright smile. It made my stomach churn. I hated Jared for even existing.

"Of course not. I am so sorry, Jess. I wish there was something I could do."

"There isn't anything."

"Can I ask you something?" I asked tentatively.

"Sure."

"If you hadn't had sex, why did you push me to sleep with Toby?"

"Push you?" Jess took in a deep breath. "Like you would let anyone push you to do something that wasn't part of your plan? Sex on your six-month anniversary with Toby fit your plan. I just told you what you wanted to hear."

"What do you mean something not in my plan? I don't have a plan."

65

"Of course you do. Straight A's in high school, all state for tennis, Princeton, marry the right guy, get the perfect job, and have 2.5 perfect children." Jess laughed but it sounded forced.

"Wow, is that really how you view me?"

"I love you, but you are not an easy friend to live up to. And look, once again I screwed up." She laughed dryly.

"You didn't screw up."

"Yes I did, don't lie to me. I messed up and now I have to live with it."

"Don't you want to at least talk to him? I mean, are you sure you don't want to see him again, you know, to get some closure or something?"

"Definitely not. It's not like I'm mad at him or anything. I wanted to sleep with him, or I thought I did, it just wasn't what I thought it would be. It wasn't what my first time was supposed to feel like. It should have been with Emmett. It's funny, isn't it? I'm with a guy for over a year and won't put out, but I end up sleeping with a virtual stranger. But it's too late and I just want to forget about what happened."

"Jess…"

"Just drop it. Please?"

"Okay," I barely whispered. "You want a ride to the airport?"

"No. You have to work. It's bad enough I'm quitting. I'll call a cab."

"You sure? I really don't mind. And stop worrying about work, it doesn't matter."

Jess nodded. "Really, I'll take a cab."

"I'm going to miss you!" I sniffled, wiping away some of my own tears. It was all happening too fast. I couldn't believe she was leaving.

"You'll be fine. Don't let what happened to me keep you from Levi. I think he might be just what you need."

"Whatever. I really couldn't care less about Levi right now."

"Just don't completely write him off. I think he's good for you. You seem to work."

"If you say so."

"Good. Now go to work."

"Don't you at least want help packing?" I asked.

"No, really, I just want to be alone."

"All right. I get it." I gave her another hug as I headed out. "Bye, Jess."

***

It wasn't until hours later when I went back up to our room after work that the reality of Jess leaving hit me. She might have been annoying at times, but she was my friend, and now I really was on my own. Dad had left me a message to let me know he'd be gone at least another week.

Feeling sorry for myself and really sad for Jess, I decided to just spend the night vegging out. I changed into lounge pants and a racer back tank, waited for the carrot cake I ordered from room

67

service, and opened up the latest chick lit on my e-reader.

I jumped up from the couch when I heard a knock on the door.

Expecting my dessert, I quickly opened the door and moved back as Levi smiled at me from the hallway.

"What are you doing here?"

Levi pushed his way into my room as I awkwardly sidestepped him. "Did you forget we had plans?"

"Plans? Oh yeah, coffee, I forgot." I tried to keep my voice even but I was so upset and angry. I walked over to the couch and pulled my knees up to my chest.

"Hey, what's going on Allie?" Levi knelt down in front of me.

"You're calling me Allie?"

"Whoa, now you are annoyed at me for calling you Allie? Can a guy ever get a break?"

I shrugged.

"Seriously, are you okay?"

"I guess, but this summer has turned into a disaster." I'm not sure what made me open up to him, but once I started I couldn't stop. "Jess left and my dad still hasn't come back. So yeah, great, I get to spend the rest of the summer all alone. Just what I needed."

"Hey, don't say you're alone. Don't I count for something?"

I looked up at Levi's million-dollar smile. I couldn't help it; I smiled back.

"That's what I was looking for. It's going to be okay. But why did Jess leave?"

"It's—" I started to say it was because of Jared but thought better of it. "It's personal"

"I'll take that, but on one condition?"

"What?"

"Come out with me tonight. I promise I'll cheer you up."

I needed a distraction and Levi was being uncharacteristically nice so I agreed. "Sure, just let me get changed."

I was about to walk into the bathroom when there was another knock on the door—room service. "Just leave it, here you go." Levi quickly took charge and I never even saw who delivered it.

He opened the Styrofoam container. "You want to eat cake first, or do you want to get changed?"

"I'm not in the mood for it anymore. You can have it or just put it in the fridge."

I took my time getting ready. Washing my face, I stared at my reflection in the mirror unable to ignore the flush I saw there. Levi had such a physical effect on me. I had never been so attracted to a guy in my life. I changed into a pair of dark jeans and a tank top. It was hot out, but I wanted the comfort of my favorite jeans. I dug out a pair of Mary Janes from my closet, needing a break from sandals.

As I brushed my hair and put on some makeup, my cell phone rang in the living area. I thought about running out to answer it, but I wasn't in the mood to talk to anyone. I dropped my brush when I heard Levi's voice from through the closed door.

"Hello."

Anger flared. Had he actually picked up my phone?

"No, Allie's not available right now, she's getting changed."

"Who am I? The name's Levi. Well, hello Toby, but I'm sorry I think Allie would have mentioned a boyfriend before she spent the night at my place. Are you sure you don't mean ex-boyfriend?"

I froze with my hand on the knob. My first reaction was to grab the phone from him, but maybe this was what Toby needed to finally take the hint that it was over.

"No, I won't go to hell, but I'll take a message." Levi laughed and I hesitated a little longer.

"You can come out now, I'm off."

I pushed open the door. "How'd you know I was listening?"

"I heard you breathing."

"You heard me through the door?"

"You didn't really think you were fooling me, did you?"

"Whatever. I can't believe you answered my phone."

"You could have stopped me at any time. Something tells me you have no problem with what I told Toby."

"You're right."

"I'm sure I am, but about what exactly?"

"That I don't mind what you said. He's my ex-boyfriend. We broke up a few months ago and he hasn't really accepted it."

"I can't say I blame him." Levi watched me, not bothering to hide his blatant evaluation of every inch of me.

"So, aren't we going out?" I asked, uncomfortable talking about Toby with Levi. It just felt wrong.

"Yes, the night awaits."

I followed Levi out into the hallway, noticing the empty cake container on the table before letting the door lock behind us.

***

Coffee with Levi was surprisingly relaxing. Maybe he felt bad for me or possibly he figured out the other tactics weren't working, but Levi was actually polite and an interesting conversationalist. He had me laughing which was something I didn't expect to do again for a while. He also showed me a slightly more serious side to him.

"What really brought you down here this summer?"

"What do you mean? Working at the hotel…"

"That's what you say, but couldn't you have gotten a job back home?"

"What does it matter?"

"I'm just trying to figure you out."

"Figure me out?"

"You have to be the hardest girl to read."

I laughed. "I can't be that hard to read."

"We have a girl with a few months before leaving for college and instead of staying home to enjoy time with her friends, either bumming around or working some silly part time job, you drive across the country to work at a hotel for a dad who has been here all of one day since you arrived."

"Get to the point." I wasn't sure where he was headed.

"Either this is all an elaborate effort to get away from your ex, or you're running from something else."

"I'm not running from anything."

"So it's all Toby?"

"No, it's not."

"Okay, so what is it?"

"Can't there be a third choice? I wanted to try something new."

"Isn't college trying something new already?" He gazed at me as if challenging me to contradict him.

"Yes, but that's different." I struggled to find the words to explain it, because I didn't completely know why I did it myself.

"Different?"

"Yeah, I don't know, it just seemed like an adventure."

"An adventure? You're looking for an adventure huh? Where do I sign up?" He wriggled an eyebrow.

I laughed. "Stop, I just mean no one would ever expect me to spend a summer in New Orleans. It's different and it was so last minute. I actually quit another job at the last second so I could come here."

Levi fake gasped. "What? How could you?"

"Well, I guess it wasn't quitting because I didn't quite start, but I was supposed to be a lifeguard at a local beach. I changed my mind when my dad called to invite me down."

"Then I propose a toast." Levi lifted his to-go coffee cup.

"A toast? With coffee?"

"You can toast with any beverage."

"Sure, why not?" I raised my cup as well. "But what are we toasting?"

"To Allie's great adventure."

I laughed as he tapped his cup to mine and dramatically finished the rest of his coffee.

My phone rang. "It's Jess. Do you mind if I get this?"

"No, not a problem."

I answered. "Hey, are you home?"

"Yeah, I got in about ten minutes ago. I wanted to apologize for leaving like that. I didn't mean to ditch you."

"It's okay, I completely understand."

A group of people walked into the coffee shop talking loudly.

"Hey, where are you?" Jess asked.

"Out getting coffee."

"With who?"

"Umm, can I call you later?"

"Wait, are you with Levi? You are, aren't you?"

"Maybe." I noticed Levi watching me, trying to figure out what was going on in our conversation.

Jess laughed. "Okay, good for you. Call me tomorrow."

"I will. Have a good night."

"You too."

I hung up, putting my phone into my back pocket. I hadn't bothered with a purse, stuffing my phone, ID, and a credit card in my jeans.

"Jess made it back?" Levi asked.

"Yeah, she just got home."

"Anything else going on?" He was obviously fishing for information.

"Nope."

Thankfully, he dropped it.

It wasn't quite 9:30 when I finished the last of my coffee. "This was actually fun. Thanks, I needed it."

"My pleasure. See, giving me a chance wasn't so bad, was it?"

"Hey, don't read too much into it. We had coffee. End of story."

"Does it have to be the end?" Levi gazed at me intently.

"What else do you have in mind?"

"Want to meet up with my friends? I bet Hailey will come if she knows you are. I think she has a girl crush on you."

"A girl crush? What are you, like three?"

"No… it's just funny. She talks about you almost as much as I do."

"I think she's pretty cool too. Definitely different from my other friends." I let the whole talking about me a lot part slide.

"Different is good, right?"

"It can be."

"Are you up for hanging out more?"

"Yeah, okay." The thought of going back to my empty room made the decision easy.

We walked through the French Quarter slowly, and I tried to take it all in. The music, the crowds, and the atmosphere still felt surreal. Music spilled out of the endless bars and clubs.

"Wow, are those people seriously dressed up as vampires?" I asked, looking in at a dark bar on the corner. Inside I watched a man and woman holding up a chalice and smiling with fangs showing.

Levi laughed. "If you think those people are weird, you'd be freaked out by the real thing."

"The real thing? Very funny."

"What, you don't think vampires are real?"

"No, and I'm glad they aren't."

"Why? Do they scare you?" Levi stopped walking, and turned me to look at him.

"Does the thought of blood sucking monsters scare me? Hell yes. Who wouldn't be scared of that?"

He laughed again even louder. "Trust me sweetheart, in New Orleans vampires are the least of your worries."

"What do you mean?" Something about the glint in his eyes made me feel a little uneasy.

Levi's face turned into a faint smile. "I'm really glad you asked that."

"What are you talking about?"

"You'll have to wait and see."

"Okay, listen, scaring me isn't a good way to get me interested, so if you have any weird tricks up your sleeve just shelve them." I wondered if this was the time to tell him I avoided horror movies like the plague.

"No tricks, hon." Levi pulled his phone out of his pocket and texted a few times.

76

I continued my people watching. I'd never seen so many middle-aged people laughing and partying before. It almost felt like the twilight zone.

Levi slipped his phone back in his pocket. "We're meeting everyone over at Club 360."

"What's that?"

"The lounge on the top of the World Trade Center down by the river."

"Okay, is it a cool view?"

"Yeah, it's got a good view." Levi laughed again and I had the distinct impression he was hiding something from me.

"You promise you aren't luring me into some trap?"

"A trap? No. Let's just call it a new experience."

My stomach dropped. What the heck did I get myself into?

Seven

The elevator doors opened on the top floor, dumping us out right at the club. As we pushed through the crowd, I felt distinctly underdressed. Things were usually very casual in New Orleans, but up there people were more dressed up.

Levi seemed to notice my discomfort. "Don't worry, we won't be here long."

"Why are we here at all then?"

"Do you ever stop asking questions?"

"I only ask this many questions when I fear for my wellbeing."

"I assure you that you are in good hands." As if to make the meaning of his words literal, Levi put his arm around my waist, pulling me tight against his side. "I see them."

We walked up to a small table in the corner overlooking the city.

"Allie! I'm so glad you came!" Hailey jumped out of her seat and hugged me.

I was thrilled to see that Hailey was also dressed casually in jeans. She wore a cropped cardigan sweater in a shade of blue that matched her eyes exactly.

"Yeah, I needed a night out."

"Where's your friend?" Jared asked casually.

"My friend? You mean Jess? She's back in New York, no thanks to you." Damn. I regretted the words as soon as they left my mouth.

"She left? What does that have to do with me?"

"Nothing. Forget I said anything." I took a seat next to Hailey.

"Okay..." Jared said giving me a look like he thought I was crazy. I doubted that Jared and I would ever get along.

I looked out the window. The skyline was lit by colorful lights that contrasted with the shadowing darkness. I could have stared at it for hours.

"All right, are you guys ready to go?" Hailey asked.

"What, already? I haven't even had a chance to enjoy the view."

"You think this is a good view? Oh, just you wait," Levi said, making everyone laugh.

"What are you talking about?"

"You sure about this, Levi? You know there is no turning back, right?" Owen asked Levi, purposely avoiding my eyes.

"Absolutely." Levi smiled making me feel even more uneasy.

Jared pushed out his chair. "Well, then let's get going, it's supposed to rain later tonight."

"Why does the rain matter?" Although the lack of information frustrated me, I couldn't deny some excitement. I loved a good surprise.

"Are you ready to find out just how far the rabbit hole goes, sweetheart?" Levi reached out his hand waiting for a response.

"Rabbit hole?" I searched for a hidden meaning in the words beyond the *Alice in Wonderland* reference, but I couldn't find one. Ignoring my unease, I went with my gut instinct. "Umm, sure?"

I accepted his hand and he led me through the crowd once more. My chest tightened with anticipation. I didn't know what Levi and his friends had in store, but I hoped it was enough to take my mind off Jess.

We walked out past the elevators and into a stairwell.

As Levi ushered me up the stairs, I realized where we were headed.

"Okay, why are we going to the roof?"

"No more questions," Levi insisted.

"But—"

Levi pressed the palm of his hand into my back gently. "No more questions."

"It's all right. We're not taking you up there to kill you." Hailey laughed but I started to question my trust in these people I hardly knew.

I thought about turning around but with Jared in front of me and Levi behind me, I didn't see too many options. I took a deep breath. "Fine."

I followed Jared out into the humid night. The lights of the city danced off the water and the colored lights of the Hibernia building created an eerie glow.

So enthralled by the view, I was surprised when I felt Levi's arms wrap around me. Through the thin fabric of my tank top, I could tell he was no longer wearing a shirt.

I struggled to turn around and he loosened his arms. I took a step back. "What the hell..." I trailed off. The guys all had their shirts off and even Hailey had shed her cardigan and was now in a thin strapped tank.

My attention first went to staring at Levi's bare muscular chest, but I quickly snapped out it.

Levi leaned over to talk to me quietly. "Now don't freak out. I promised you I wouldn't hurt you and I always keep my promises."

"Are you guys in a cult of something? Because if you are, I'm really not interested. I won't tell anyone anything, but if you don't mind I'm leaving." My thoughts returned to the *Alice in Wonderland* reference, and I wondered if they were on drugs.

"Chill out!" Jared yelled as his eyes changed from brown to solid black just like they had that first night in Jackson Square. Evidently, it wasn't a drunken illusion.

"Don't talk to her like that," Levi said with authority and Jared visibly relaxed, his eyes slowly returning to normal. Weird.

"We're not a cult. It's more like a very special society," Hailey explained taking a few steps toward me.

"A special society?"

"Maybe it would be better if we just showed her," Owen said giving me a reassuring smile. "You were sure you wanted this Levi, so there is no turning back."

Owen walked over to the edge of the building and raised a hand in a small wave before taking a backwards step and disappearing from sight.

"Oh my god! What the hell? Did he just kill himself?" I started shaking, I felt the tears splashing down my face.

"Owen's fine," Hailey said before jumping off with Jared right behind her. I knew with sickening certainty I would be getting off the building the same way.

I started to pray. It was probably the first prayer I had said in at least five years but it came automatically.

Closing my eyes, I tried to block it all out. Convinced I was about to die, I was only partly aware of Levi's arms around me.

"You said you wanted an adventure," he said quietly, teasingly, as he tightened his hold.

My stomach dropped out as an intense and complete feeling of weightlessness engulfed me. The wind stung my face as memories flooded my mind. I thought of my parents, of all the things I wanted to tell them but never did, my friends from home, and the experiences I longed for. Quickly my thoughts changed to more recent memories, to Levi.

"Open your eyes," he whispered, somehow knowing my eyes were clenched shut.

Against my better judgment, I listened. The scream died in my throat as we hurtled toward the water that had been so beautiful from the roof above.

Just when I was sure we were going to crash, we started gliding horizontally to the water for a moment before heading further away. I didn't close my eyes. As completely terrified and confused as I was, there was no way I was going to spend the last few moments of my life with my eyes closed. I was only vaguely aware as my feet hit solid ground again.

I stumbled away from Levi and fell down to the grass below me, grabbing on to the slightly damp strands as if they were my only anchor to the world. I hesitated to look up, terrified of what might be awaiting me.

Catching my first glimpse of them, my jaw dropped and my voice cracked before I could get words out. Giant black wings extended from each of their backs nearly blocking out the moonlight. "What the hell are you? Oh-my-god you're angels, aren't you? I'm dead. I'm actually dead?"

Levi laughed, making the large black wings move slightly, the effect only made him appear more frightening. "Do you really think I'm an angel?"

"A fallen angel?" I asked, grasping for a way to understand what stood in front of me. I peered around Levi to Hailey, most surprised to see her wings; the contrast of the black with her red hair was intense.

Levi laughed again. "We're not angels of any sort." He took a step closer to me.

"Then what are you?" I scooted back slowly, closing my eyes, hoping that when I opened them again there would be normal people standing in front of me.

"Open your eyes, sweetheart." Levi's hands were on my shoulders urging me to obey him. "Open your eyes."

"No, this has to be some messed up dream."

"It's not a dream."

"Yes, it is."

"No, it's not. Accept it already." It was Jared's bluntness that made me open my eyes again.

My words of anger died on my lips when I was faced once again with four sets of black wings.

"If this isn't a dream, then what are you? What's going on?"

"We're Pterons," Hailey said gently.

"Pterons?" I asked, repeating the unfamiliar word.

"We're shifters, Allie," Levi said almost as gently as Hailey. He was trying to put me at ease but I knew I was shaking.

"Shifters? Like what, a werewolf?"

Jared laughed. "We're not like werewolves. That's like saying humans are like chimps."

"Humans? Wait, because you guys aren't human…"

"Like I said, we're shifters. At one time our people shifted into crows but over time we became more of a hybrid. It's more efficient," Levi explained

"Like natural selection or something?" I said absently. Biology was my favorite subject in high school.

"Something like that." Levi kneeled down next to me and picked up my hands. "You okay?"

"I'm not sure," I said honestly.

"It really doesn't change anything." Hailey took a few steps closer to where I sat with Levi.

"You're standing there with giant wings coming out of your back, yet you tell me that nothing has changed?"

"What she means is that we're still the same people you wanted to hang out with in the beginning of the night, just *enhanced*," Owen said with a small smile.

"Enhanced? So other than flying, what can you do?"

"Other than flying?" Levi chortled. "Yes, because flying is so commonplace. But to answer your question we have some other skills, but I think this is enough for tonight."

"Oh," I said, finally at a loss of words, not sure how I was even managing to form coherent thoughts.

"You're funny, you know that?" Levi smiled, and tried to help me to my feet but I pulled back.

"Umm, can you put those things away?"

"Those *things*? Our wings? Yes, we can put them away."

I watched in awe as Levi's wings retracted like they were never there in the first place.

"Turn around," I said as I stood up.

Levi obliged and I ran my hands over his back feeling only the faintest hint of two lines. I squinted in the moonlight to see the barely perceptible raised marks.

"Are you done manhandling Levi yet or are we going to stay here all night?"

"Shut up, Jared," Hailey snapped.

"She can manhandle me all she wants." Levi turned around to face me again. "You ready to go home or do you want to see more?"

The answer was simple. "I'm ready to go home." I was still trying to process the craziness of the night.

"We'll see you tomorrow, right?" Hailey asked and I sensed some real fear in her words. She really wanted to see me again.

"Yeah, sure," I said automatically but uncertain of whether I'd keep my word.

"All right, if you're sure." Levi turned me around and wrapped his arms around me.

"Wait, stop!" Levi let go, and I turned to look at him. "I never said I wanted to fly again. How far are we from the hotel?"

"Oh, right. We can get a cab."

"No. I can get a cab. Where are we?"

"We're at the levee. You sure you don't want me to take you home? At least let me walk you to the street."

"All right, fair enough." As freaked out as I was, walking alone in the dark wasn't on the top of my to-do list.

A cab was waiting by the time we reached the road, and I assumed someone else had called one for me.

"Good night," Levi said quietly with a quick wave as I opened the door and slid inside. I smiled lightly as the cab pulled away. Looking out the window as we drove through the streets of the French Quarter, I thought over the events of the night trying to make myself believe they were real.

Eight

The only hint that any of my memories from the night before were real came in the form of five angry voicemails from Toby waiting for me when I woke up. At least I knew Levi had been in my suite.

The messages themselves were actually a bit comical at first. Toby was furious in the first one, asking me where I got the nerve to hook up with a hillbilly. I had to laugh, Levi a hillbilly? By the fourth one, Toby seemed to have changed his approach. He was begging me to forgive him for jumping to conclusions because obviously it was just a big misunderstanding. The last one was kind of sad. He had heard Jess was home and asked why I didn't leave too. I realized how odd it was that the thought of returning home didn't even cross my mind. Being alone in New Orleans wasn't ideal, but neither was giving up before the summer ended.

I deleted the last message and didn't even consider calling Toby back. I had enough to process and talking to Toby wasn't going to help. I also had a message from Jess so I called her back, but I got her voicemail.

I didn't have to work which meant the whole day was open. I took an obscenely long shower, trying to comb through my memories. As odd as they were, I knew it had to be real. Somehow, it just fit. I knew that I was supposed to be freaked out by it. I had just discovered that the guy I was into was actually a paranormal creature. I guess I don't have normal reactions because once the shock of it all wore off, it was really cool. I mean, there was something undeniably sexy and exciting about Levi's wings and the power I knew came with them. It took bad boy to a whole new level. Hanging out with him was definitely not in "my plans" as Jess had described my mapped out life.

Pulling on a jean skirt and pink tank, I quickly finished getting ready. With no real plans, I stared at my phone willing it to ring. I had never been the girl waiting for a guy to call, but part of me needed to know that Levi was still interested and that the previous night had been more than a tease.

I glanced at my phone one last time around 11:00 a.m. as I walked into the hall, determined to stop waiting around.

"Hoping for a call from someone?"

I smiled when I noticed Levi leaning against the wall.

"How long have you been out here?"

"Awhile." He straightened up and took a step towards me.

"Oh. You could have knocked…" I trailed off.

"I figured there was no need to push you anymore than I did last night. But I had to see you—to see if you were still reacting well," Levi said carefully, like he was treading on thin ice.

"Why wouldn't I be reacting well?" I asked with a smile.

"It's not every day that you see something like that. Maybe in my life, but not yours."

"I guess it would be normal in yours."

He smiled. "Any chance I can take you to a late breakfast?"

"That depends. How are we getting there?" I asked, not sure what answer I wanted to hear.

Levi laughed. "We're walking, but would you want to fly with me again?"

I tried to dial down my real level of excitement at the thought of it. "I could be persuaded."

He reached over and ran a finger down my cheek. "I'm glad. There's more I want to show you."

"So are we going to go now or—"

"Uh, it's broad daylight Al, don't you think someone would notice?"

"Oh, you only fly at night? And now you're calling me Al?"

"We usually only fly at night, but there are exceptions I'm not getting into right now. And I am still trying to settle on what name I like best."

"Doesn't my opinion count?"

Levi moved toward me, practically pinning me against the wall. "Your opinion always counts, but I already told you I'm not calling you what everyone else does. I'm going to have my own name for you."

"What, like you name a pet? That sounds kind of possessive."

"It is kind of possessive, Al." He winked and took my hand leading me down the hall. "Have you been to Café du Monde yet?"

I shook my head.

"Good, let's go." Still holding my hand, Levi led us to the elevator. We stopped several times to let other people on, but Levi never once took his eyes off me.

Billy was waiting by the front entrance as we walked out. "Hey Allie, I haven't seen you or Jess today, where have you been hiding?"

"Jess went back to New York," I said cautiously, hoping to avoid a long discussion. If Jess ever felt like talking to Billy again she had his number.

"Oh. She really left? Did you ever find out what was going on with her?" Billy didn't bother to hide the disappointment in his voice.

"Personal reasons." I shrugged. "I'll see you around."

Levi nodded stiffly to Billy as we walked outside into the bright light of the sun.

Jackson Square looked different in the daylight. Still filled with artists and musicians, it lacked the intensity it held at night. The place was full of tourists snapping pictures of the large St. Louis Cathedral. I looked around, taking it all in.

"There's nothing quite like New Orleans, huh?" Levi acknowledged my perusal.

"Not really. I mean it has a similar feel to Paris, but it definitely has a flavor all of its own." I smiled realizing that a lot of that flavor had to do with the guy standing next to me. It was easy to forget he was anything other than a frat boy type, but Levi had let me in on his secret and now I knew there was a lot more than muscles hiding underneath his tight white t-shirt.

I shook myself from my blatant ogling when Levi laughed. "You still interested in breakfast?" The question reminded me of the last time he offered it up and I knew there was at least the hint of an innuendo there.

"Absolutely." I held his gaze and I could tell it surprised him. I still don't think Levi was used to a girl he couldn't fluster.

Slipping under the green and white awning, Levi pulled out a chair for me at a round table. He waited until I was seated before sitting across from me. The table was small, especially for someone as tall as Levi and his legs brushed against mine anytime he moved.

Levi asked for two orders of beignets and a chicory coffee for each of us. The server brought the coffee immediately, and we sipped in comfortable silence until breakfast arrived. The beignets were sweet and hot, and I had to laugh at myself as I got the white powdered sugar all over myself.

"Wow, these are good!"

"What isn't there to like about fried dough covered in sugar?" Levi said playfully but I could tell he was glad to see me having fun.

"So, Princeton, huh?" he asked, leaning back in his chair.

"Yup. Home of the Tigers."

He laughed, nearly choking on a sip of his coffee. "Yeah, because that's what comes to mind first when someone says Princeton."

"What comes to mind for you?"

"Oh, I don't know. How about uptight preps who wouldn't know how to have a good time if it bit them on the ass?"

"Ouch. You don't think I know how to have fun?"

"On the contrary hon, I know you can have fun. It's the others I'm worried about. I'm afraid that next time I see you you'll be a walking Ralph Lauren ad."

I was suddenly glad that I'd decided against the pink polo dress I had almost thrown on. "What makes you think you'll ever see me after this summer?"

"You've had your taste Al. Even if you leave in August, you'll be back for more."

"And what are you referring to exactly?"

"The city." He paused to look at me. "Of course."

"Of course. If you're done, it's my turn."

"Your turn for what?" he asked.

"To ask a question."

"I wasn't aware we were taking turns."

I didn't bother to acknowledge his comment. "So, you're graduating this year, right?" He nodded. "What's next for you?"

"Uh, taking over the family business." He looked away as he answered and I knew I had struck a nerve.

"Which is?"

"You asked your question."

"Whoa, are there more secrets?" You would think that after revealing his wings there wouldn't be much more to hide.

"It's kind of hard to explain. Let's just say it's a leadership position."

"You're not going to elaborate?"

"My turn." He evaded me.

"Fine."

"So, what's the story with Toby?"

"What do you mean? I already told you he's my ex."

"Yeah, but why is he your ex?"

"Why do you even care?"

"Eh, just curiosity."

"And why would I indulge that curiosity when you evaded my question?"

"My good looks?" He took a slow sip of his coffee.

"Very funny. Really there isn't much to tell. We dated about a year, and we worked but I got tired of the lack of sparks. I brought up my concerns and he brushed them off, so I broke up with him." I tried to play it off nonchalantly, but it hadn't been a painless breakup. Toby took it hard, and as much as I knew we weren't meant to be, we had a lot of history that was hard to let go of.

"Lack of sparks? You're looking for passion then?"

I felt heat rising to my cheeks and hoped I could stop it. I was not the girl who blushed. "Okay, my turn again. What's with Jared and Owen?"

"What do you mean?" Levi asked.

"You act like girls or something. You're never apart."

"They're not here now."

"I get this vibe that they answer to you or something. Does this have to do with the 'family business'?"

"Maybe."

"Seriously? You're evading my question again?"

"And here I thought girls liked a man of mystery." Clearly, he was unwilling to answer the question.

I groaned. "On that note, are you ready to get going?"

"Sure." He threw some cash down on the table and we got up to leave.

I stopped to dust some powdered sugar off my skirt. "So, where to now?"

"Where do you want to go?"

"Hmm, I don't know."

"What would you be doing if you were home?"

"I'd probably be at the beach," I confessed, picturing how good the cool water would feel. "It's pretty much my favorite place to be."

"I'll have to keep that in mind. The beach is a little hard to give you right now, but how about we check out the French Market?"

"Shopping?"

"Is that a problem?"

"Not at all, I am just surprised by the suggestion," I admitted.

"It's not like I'm taking you to the mall."

"True, but you don't seem like the shopping type."

"If you're done complaining…" he trailed off with a hint of a smile.

"Lead the way." I gestured him forward with my hand.

The French Market provided some much-needed shade. After several weeks, I was still no more used to the heat and humidity of the city. Not that summer in New York was particularly pleasant, but New Orleans was on a whole different level.

We weren't the only ones visiting the market, and I guessed it was the usual Saturday crowd.

"I think I remember now why I don't come here much," Levi mumbled.

"Not one for crowds?" I asked.

"Not really. You?"

"I actually kind of like them. I think it's why I like New York City so much. I love the feeling of getting lost in a big crowd."

"I learn something new about you every day," he joked, guiding us down the center aisle.

"I think you won that contest last night." I smiled, thinking about just how much I had learned. "Well, we can leave if you want."

"Not until we do one thing."

"Okay…"

"You like sweets, right?" he asked.

"Of course."

"Loretta's has some great pralines you've got to try."

Levi stepped into a small store within the market. I stood back watching the crowd move by as I waited for him to finish his purchase.

"Ready?" Levi took my hand leading me out of the market back the way we came. He never let go of my hand, and I didn't fight it. Something had changed the night before. I had seen a hint of the real Levi and I wanted more. We passed back through Jackson Square and I never bothered to ask where we were going. I ate my praline, enjoying my breakfast of treats.

Levi came to a stop in front of a large building that appeared to be an old brewery. "The view here isn't quite as good as last night, but it's pretty nice."

I noticed the sign hanging in front of the door. "Pat O's?"

"It's Pat O's on the River, good drinks and a nice view."

"Drinks in the middle of the afternoon?"

"You're in N'awlins Al, get used to it."

He led me inside and up in the elevator. We walked through the indoor bar and out onto the patio.

"Hi Levi," a busty waitress called as we headed outside. She watched him eagerly waiting for his response.

Levi barely nodded in acknowledgement. I smiled without meaning to.

We took seats at a high top table overlooking the river.

"You weren't kidding, this is a great view." I settled back into my chair, thankful for the awning overhead.

"I thought you would like it. You seem to really like good views."

"The usual?" a waiter asked as he approached the table.

"Yes and a hurricane for her."

"All right, be right out with those."

"Does everyone who works here know you?" I asked.

"Not *everyone*." He smiled.

"Well anyway, what did you order me?"

"You'll like it. It's pretty much the signature drink of the city and the specialty drink here, so you need to have it at least once."

"Is it as good as the other drink you keep buying me?"

"Maybe not as good, but you'll still enjoy it."

"What did you get?"

"Whiskey."

"How do you know I wouldn't prefer that?"

"I don't take you as the type to take your liquor straight." He watched me, daring me to contradict him.

I contemplated arguing, but that would have ended in me drinking whisky, and that wasn't something that sounded remotely appealing. "You're right. I was just asking."

The waiter brought our drinks over. I took a sip and Levi was right; I did like it. It was sweet but still had something to it. "Ah, it's such a gorgeous afternoon."

Levi laughed lightly. "I'm glad to see you enjoying yourself."

"Is there any chance you'll take me—" The blare of a barge drowned me out. "Any chance you'll—" It happened again and I decided to wait.

"What were you asking?" He seemed genuinely interested.

"Any chance of a repeat performance from last night?" I finally got out.

"You liked that, huh?"

99

"Yeah, I can't say I've ever had a ride like that before."

A middle-aged woman at the table next to us coughed, evidently misinterpreting our conversation. Levi must have realized it too. "Sure baby, I'll take you for a ride anytime."

I smacked his leg under the table.

"Ouch."

"You so deserved that."

"You're the one that wants the ride." He tried unsuccessfully to stifle a laugh.

I ignored his last statement. "Is that a yes? You'll take me again?"

"Of course, I have no intentions of letting you down."

We finished our drinks, enjoying the view and talking about nothing in particular. If Levi's plan had been to continue distracting me from thinking about Jess, he was very successful.

Nine

After some more sightseeing and a late dinner, we headed uptown to Levi's place. His apartment was as immaculate as the last time. Owen and Jared sat on the couch playing some kind of war video game. They stopped screaming at each other and the game long enough to acknowledge me with a few grunts.

"Can I get you anything?" Levi asked as I glanced around. More awake this time, I noticed a couple of black and white photographs of street scenes on the wall. I made a mental note to find out who the photographer of the group was.

"I'm fine, but thanks."

"Want a tour?"

"A tour? Is there really that much more to see?"

"Of course there is. You never even saw my room last time." He looked at me mischievously as he took off through the kitchen into a hallway.

"You probably remember that's Jared's room," Levi pointed. "Owen's is over there and I'm here on the end." Levi walked into the room he indicated as his own.

His room was much larger than I expected, with a king size bed pushed against the back wall. "Wow, you don't see too many beds that big in college apartments."

"How many college apartments have you been in? Didn't you just graduate high school?"

"I have older friends…"

"Older friends who like to show you their bedrooms with inadequately sized beds? Good to know."

I decided to ignore him and check out the rest of the room. Unlike the main living space, his room was a mess. Dirty laundry mixed with books on the hardwood floor. Piles of clothes cluttered the top of his dresser, his desk and even the desk chair.

"So is it Owen who keeps the rest of this place clean? I mean, obviously it's not you."

"You automatically assume it's Owen?"

"Yeah… wait, don't tell me it's Jared."

"Okay, I won't."

"Wow, Jared the neat freak," I said with surprise.

"You're not his biggest fan, are you?"

"No, not at all," I admitted.

"It has something to do with your friend, doesn't it?"

My defenses went up immediately. "I don't want to talk about Jess, okay?"

"Sure, but Jared's not all bad."

"If you say so."

"I do. He's had my back since we were kids, and I think he kind of grows on you." He paused. "Do you still want to fly?"

"Yes!" I quickly forgot I was annoyed at him.

"All right, let me talk to the guys, be right back."

Levi left me standing alone in his room so I continued my perusal. I refrained from invading his privacy, half out of politeness and half out of fear he'd catch me. What kind of stuff did a not quite human guy have in his room? I sat down on the edge of his unmade bed, kicking away a gray Tulane sweatshirt with my flip-flop.

Levi returned before my curiosity could get the best of me. "All right, they're in. Owen's going to call Hailey and have her meet us."

"Where are we going exactly?"

"It's a surprise."

"What if I don't like surprises?" I asked.

"Come on, Al, you like surprises." Levi leaned over, placing a hand on either side of me on his bed.

"What makes you say that?"

"I just know." He placed a feather light kiss on my lips. Instead of continuing the kiss as I expected, he straightened up and headed toward his door. He pulled off his t-shirt, throwing it down carelessly before grabbing the hoodie sweatshirt from the floor. "First I can't get you into my room, and now I can't get you out of it?"

"Shut up." I got up and followed him into the hallway, trying to ignore my disappointment at his quick departure.

Owen and Jared were waiting for us by the open front door, also shirtless.

"Put this on." Levi tossed me the sweatshirt.

"You want me to wear something that was in a ball on the floor?"

"It's clean. I just did laundry."

"So why was it on the floor?"

Owen laughed.

"Just put it on. We're not going high, but it's a longer flight and it's going to be cold."

"No thanks."

"Fine, suit yourself. But at least bring it with you; you'll thank me when you're freezing later."

"Somehow I doubt that, but I'll bring it."

"All right, you ready?" Levi asked.

"Definitely." I was ready for my adrenaline fix.

Levi chuckled. "Wow, you really are pumped up for this."

"Why? Do most girls not react this way?"

"Most girls? How many girls do you think I've flown before?"

"I'd assume quite a few."

"Naw, Allie, you're his first. Isn't that sweet? Okay, end of story, let's go," Jared said impatiently.

"Seriously? Then why'd you take me?" Levi's decision to let me in on his world now seemed even bigger.

"It felt right. Let's get out of here. Oh, you might want to hold those flip-flops."

I followed the guys down the front porch, and around to the side of the house. When Levi

104

stopped, I took off my flip-flops, enfolding them in the sweatshirt I was already holding.

Levi turned me around before wrapping his arms around my waist. "Have fun."

I stifled a scream as we took off again. I obviously knew he was going to do it, but the sensation was still shocking.

The city moved by in a blur as Levi swept down low enough to keep the skyline in view. With only his arms protecting me, I easily could have fallen, but I knew that Levi wasn't going to drop me. The feeling of safety in his arms was incredible. Still, flying was a huge adrenaline rush, putting any roller coaster to shame. The city lights started disappearing as the ocean came into view in the distance.

Levi fell back behind the others, likely sensing how much I was enjoying myself. We followed the beach until we landed gently on the sand. I ran my hands down my arms, trying to warm myself up. Levi laughed, giving me a look that said, "I told you so."

"Why don't you get cold when you fly?" I asked, admiring his shirtless chest.

"My body's designed for it, yours isn't."

"Oh, I guess that makes sense."

After taking a moment to regain my balance and warm up, I reveled in the feeling of the sand beneath my toes. We were close enough to the water to hear the waves lapping at the shore. "I can't believe you brought me to a beach."

"You like it?"

"I love it. But where are we?"

"Grand Isle."

"I've never heard of it, but it's nice to know there's a beach so close." We walked over to join the others.

Hailey added kindling to a roaring bonfire before turning to smile at me. "I'm so glad you weren't scared away."

"Me too." The fire was the only source of light, and I craned my neck to watch the stars.

"Be honest, you love it." Levi slipped an arm around my waist. "You're the one who asked me to take you flying again."

"Nice, it's pretty cool right?" Hailey's face lit up and I realized how worried she must have been. Letting me in on their secret had been a big risk for all of them, and she had every reason to assume I'd freak out.

"Very. It's, uh, definitely different, but I like different."

***

After sitting around the fire for at least an hour, Levi leaned in to whisper to me, "Want to take a walk?"

"Sounds good," I got up, giving a small wave to the others.

We walked off into the darkness, my hand firmly in Levi's larger one. It's funny how quickly I got comfortable with it. Tugging on his hand to get him to follow, I headed down closer to the water.

I breathed in a breath of ocean air. "There is nothing like the beach at night."

"You like it at night, too? I was worried you wouldn't like it without the sun."

"I like the beach during the day, but I love it at night. There is just something about listening to the waves in the darkness and the soft glow of the stars reflecting off the water."

"Yeah. It's nice." Levi's voice came from right behind me, close to my ear. I leaned back into him, and he wrapped his arms around me. We stood that way for a while before he turned me towards him.

In the glimmering of the moonlight Levi studied me, his eyes staring into mine like he was trying to read me. "You're so beautiful. So unbelievably beautiful..." he trailed off as his lips met mine.

The kiss started off gentle but neither of us could keep it that way for long. It might have been our second kiss, but it was our first real one. I realized quickly that the first time at the bar we had both been holding back. Levi deepened the kiss, his arms tightening around me before lowering me down onto the sand.

We were just close enough to the surf that the sand was damp beneath the bare skin of my shoulders and legs, but it didn't matter—all thoughts were on Levi. With ragged breaths, he kept his weight braced while leaning down over me. He traced his fingers over my stomach, pushing up the bottom of my tank top. I couldn't get enough of his touch.

Closing my eyes, I melted into him, oblivious to any thoughts of what I was doing. Running my fingers down his muscular back, I paused on the two tiny lines. I moved my exploration further down his back and he groaned.

He shifted me slightly, pulling away briefly to remove my tank. He came back, trailing kisses from my ear to my neck, his fingers on the straps of my bra.

I didn't hear the approaching footsteps.

"Are you guys ever coming back? Oh wow, leaving now," Hailey stammered.

Crossing my arms across my chest, I sat up snapping out of my daze.

"Wait, no Hailey. It's not what you think." Pulling my tank over my head, I got up to follow her as she hurried away.

I turned to glance back at Levi, sitting completely unapologetically on the sand. "If it wasn't what she thought, then what was it?"

"Almost a mistake," I mumbled before hurrying after Hailey.

"It didn't seem like you were worried about that a minute ago!" he shouted after me.

"I'm really sorry you had to see that." Catching up to Hailey, I decided to assess the damage. I didn't want her to think I was just some groupie girl, willing to hook up with Levi now that I knew what he was.

"You don't have to explain. I actually think it's kind of cute."

"Cute?"

"Yeah… I don't know, I think you guys work together…" Hailey trailed off as we joined Jared and Owen by the fire. After giving us a few feet of space Levi caught up as well. It was funny; Jess had also described us as "working."

"Nice of you two to join us," Owen jested.

"It would have been nicer had we not, but what can you do." Levi shrugged, the frustrated expression on his face contradicting his nonchalant tone.

I groaned, eliciting laughter from everyone else.

"Relax, no one cares that you are finally done playing hard to get." Jared had to open his mouth again.

"Oh, I wasn't playing at anything." He was seriously getting on my nerves. "What's your problem?"

"My problem?" he asked with mock innocence.

"Yeah. Why can't you go five minutes without saying something obnoxious to me?"

Owen snorted.

I glanced at Levi to make sure he wasn't going to try to get involved. Thankfully, he just stood crossing his arms with an amused expression.

"Like you're any better. You can't even look me in the eye tonight."

"Yes, I can." I walked over to him, stopping only inches away, and stared him down. "See. I can look you in the eye."

"Levi, can you tell your girl to heel?" Jared said dryly before turning away and disappearing down the beach.

"Arggh! What the hell is his problem?" I yelled to no one in particular.

"Isn't it obvious?" Owen answered.

I turned to look at him. "What's obvious?"

"You took his wing man away."

"Oh, please!" Hailey laughed. "Jared is just being his annoying self."

I looked over at Levi to get his take, but he just shrugged. "I'll talk to him if you want, but you seem perfectly capable of handling it yourself."

"Yes, I am. And anyway, I should really be getting back."

"Already?" Levi asked watching me.

"Yeah, it's getting late. I have something called work tomorrow. Ever heard of it?" I snapped, still angry with Jared.

"What, you think I don't have a job?"

I realized I had no idea whether he did or not. "Do you?"

"I work for my father too."

"Oh."

"See, we have even more in common than you thought." He smiled.

The smile was enough to curb my anger and move my thoughts to happier places, like what almost happened on the sand. I suppressed a smile of my own.

"All right, I'll take you home."

"Good seeing you." Hailey tossed my flip-flops over to me from where I'd dropped them in the sand. I caught them before pulling the hoodie over my head, this time heeding Levi's advice.

"You look too good in that," Levi said, taking me in wearing his oversized sweatshirt. He moved behind me and pulled me into his arms.

"Bye!" I called to Hailey and Owen just as Levi took off.

As weird as it sounds, I was slowly getting used to flying. It was definitely one of those things that didn't lose its appeal the more you did it. Instead, any fear disappeared and the intensity increased.

Landing on my balcony, Levi jimmied the door open. "This was an interesting night."

"Did you just break into my room?" I asked as he opened the door.

"Yeah, but the lock will still work, I promise."

"Except for one key problem."

"Which is?" he asked.

"It won't keep you out."

"Like you want that, babe."

I groaned. "Do you realize how frustrating you are?"

"Of course I do, but I like you all flustered and hot."

"Okay, shut up and get out of here."

"No goodnight kiss? Maybe a night cap?" he teased.

As badly as I wanted to feel his lips on mine again, if I planned to spend the night alone I needed him to leave—immediately.

"Goodnight, Levi."

He shrugged. "Oh well, see you in your dreams."

Before I could come up with a snappy retort, he was gone.

"So much for swearing off men," I said quietly as I closed the balcony door behind me.

Ten

Morning came entirely too soon. I hit snooze on my alarm twice before dragging myself out of bed and into the shower. Thankfully, the hot water did the trick and after a quick breakfast, I made it down before my 9:00 a.m. shift.

The desk was relatively quiet at first, and I took the chance to talk to Natalie about Jess's sudden departure. I hoped it wouldn't mess up the schedule too much. Prepared to offer to pick up extra shifts, I filled her in.

"It's fine. You two were doubling up all the time anyway, so the only difference now is that we won't be paying two people to do the same job."

"Oh." I hadn't thought about how inefficient it was to have Jess and I working together all the time. I guess I took it for granted.

"Is everything okay though? It seemed like she was enjoying it here up until the past few days."

I hesitated, contemplating my answer. "Yeah, I think she just needed to get home."

"I see. Well, I hope you still manage to have fun without her. I know the two of you are close."

"I'll be fine. I'm sure my dad will be back soon anyway."

"I'm sure you're right," Natalie agreed even though she probably knew just how unlikely that was.

I walked back to the main desk where a small line of irritated guests waited to be helped. I put on a smile and helped check out the first couple. The one nice thing about how busy we were is that the morning moved quickly. Later on, Billy came over to hang out at the desk. He was definitely still disappointed about Jess leaving.

"She's definitely not coming back?" he asked.

"No, I think she's planning to just stay home until school starts."

"That's too bad. Tell her I said hi if you talk to her. Okay?"

"Sure." As I agreed I thought about what it would it be like when I finally saw Jess again. It's not like she left because of me, but somehow I knew that our friendship would never be the same. I only hoped it survived. As imperfect as our friendship was, I didn't want to lose it.

"Oh, look it's your friend." Billy's sarcastic remark brought me out of my thoughts.

I looked across the lobby to glimpse Levi flanked on either side by guys in suits. He glanced up at me but didn't acknowledge me at all. I watched as he headed to the elevator, trying to quell my annoyance that he hadn't even smiled. I reminded myself that I had no reason to expect more from him than some fun nights out. Besides, I was the one to rebuff him the night before. Maybe I had denied him one too many times.

Evidently noticing my disappointment, Billy awkwardly patted my shoulder. "Ouch. Sorry about that, Allie."

"Oh, I don't care. It's not like we're really together or anything."

"Who aren't you really together with?" Alex strolled in and I realized it was already time for the bar to open.

"Oh, no one important."

"Allie's been hanging out with one of *them*, you know that all important one, and he just snubbed her," Billy explained.

"Well, it's better that way. I already told you to stay away from those guys; really there is something so off about them."

In all of the craziness of the past week, I had pushed Alex's warning out of my head, even if I had thought about the basement once or twice. "There you go, lecturing me again."

"I'm just looking out for you."

"Sure you are," I smiled before excusing myself to go through some papers. I made sure to stay busy the rest of the morning.

By lunchtime, I decided that as much fun as I had hanging out with Levi, I needed to take a break. The hurt I felt at his remoteness made me realize that I was moving into caring too much territory. The whole reason I had sworn off men was to avoid that kind of drama.

Natalie came out of her office around noon. "Hey, you want to grab some lunch?"

"Yeah, sure." I jumped at the opportunity. I needed to cool my thoughts, and some lunch conversation sounded like a good cure.

We decided to eat right at the hotel restaurant to save time. Over Cajun chicken salads, we shared some small talk.

"Are you from around here?" I asked.

"I'm originally from Baton Rouge. I moved to New Orleans after college and never left."

"Do you have any family around here?"

"I have some cousins in the city, but my parents and brothers are still in Baton Rouge."

"Oh, okay, at least that's not so far."

"Very true. Do you miss your mom?" she asked.

"Yeah, definitely. But this is good practice for starting school in the fall. Even though I'm only going to be about two hours away, I don't want to be that girl who goes home all the time."

"Hey, I went to college in the same city I'm from and it was still a hard adjustment. There is nothing wrong with needing to see your mom once in a while."

"I know; it's more the principle."

Natalie paused, like she was choosing her words carefully. "If I can give you any advice about starting college, it's that you need to do what's right for you and ignore what anyone else thinks, because in the end you are the only one who has to live your life."

I thought over her words. "Thanks Natalie, I'll keep that in mind."

"And if you ever need someone to talk to, feel free to call. It hasn't been that long since I was in your shoes."

"Thanks, that's really nice of you to offer."

"You ready to get back to work?"

"Sure. Thanks for lunch, it was fun."

"We need to do this more often." She smiled.

After lunch, the afternoon crawled. Waiting for the clock to hit five signaling the end of my workday, I happened to be staring at the elevators when Levi walked back into the lobby, this time alone. Noticing my gaze, he smiled and waved in greeting before heading over. As tempted as I was to disappear into the back office and avoid him, I wasn't going to run.

"Hello there, beautiful. How was your day?" Levi leaned an elbow against the counter directly in front of me. I glanced across the way to see Alex staring at us from the bar.

"It was work; I had a nice lunch though."

"Did you have company for this nice lunch or was it solo?"

"I had company." I decided to let him draw his own conclusions and eyed Alex over Levi's head, giving his stare right back to him. Levi turned around to see what held my attention.

Scowling, Levi drew in a breath. He evidently thought my lunch was with Alex, and I decided not to correct his assumption.

"Do you want to hang out tonight?"

"No, thanks." I turned to head into the office.

A hand on my shoulder made me jump. I had expected Levi to take the hint and leave, not follow me back. Obviously, I was delusional. This was Levi.

"Am I missing something? What's up?"

"You're not actually allowed back here you know."

Ignoring my statement, he asked again. "Why don't you want to hang out? I thought you had fun yesterday."

"Yeah, it was fun. But that doesn't mean I want to hang out every night."

"Okay, what happened? Is it him?" Levi asked pointing at Alex.

"No!"

Levi visibly relaxed. "Then what is it?"

"Why does there have to be a reason? Is it that impossible to believe that I'm not interested?"

"You are interested. Don't bother to deny it. You weren't faking it on the beach."

"Could you lower your voice?" I hissed, wishing that Levi could be more discreet.

"Wait, this isn't about this morning is it?"

"Well..."

"Oh, I can explain that. I told you I work for my dad, those men I was with are his advisors. I figured you didn't need to meet them."

"Oh..." I felt lame for caring so much but I wasn't really ready to accept such a flimsy excuse. Still, I certainly wasn't going to let him know that it bothered me.

"But wow, I'm flattered that it got to you."

"Don't push it," I warned.

"So... tonight?"

I crossed my arms, trying to disguise my hurt with anger. "No thanks."

"Wait, I thought we cleared everything up?"

"It doesn't really matter. I still don't feel like going out."

"Then we can stay in... I can bring over some DVDs, or we could order something."

"You want to stay in and watch a movie?"

"Sure, why not? Besides, it's a good excuse to get into your room." He grinned slyly.

"As tempting as it sounds, I'm going to pass."

He sighed in frustration. "Okay, then what are you doing tomorrow morning?"

"I'm working..."

"Could you get out of it?"

"Depends on what for." Despite myself, I was intrigued.

"It's another surprise, but this time wear jeans and tennis shoes."

"Where would we go that I would need those?"

"You'll see." Kissing me on the cheek, he left without waiting for my answer. I wondered what I had gotten myself into.

***

I might have agreed to spend the next day with Levi, but my curiosity wasn't satisfied. I now knew that he wasn't quite human, but he still hadn't mentioned anything about the hotel. Between the lack of information and the way he blew me off, I needed answers. So far, everything about the Pterons seemed amazing, but a part of me feared he was still hiding something.

Getting into the elevator to head up to my room, I pushed the button for the basement, but like Billy had explained it did nothing. I didn't know much about elevators, but there was definitely a slot for a key card. Maybe you needed a card to gain access. I figured Dad could get me that access if I wanted. I gave him a call when I reached my room.

"Why would you need to get down there?" Dad asked. I could barely hear him over the loud voices in the background. Then I heard a door slam and it got quiet.

"Oh, I'm just trying to learn the lay of the building. You know, get a better grasp of the property."

"Oh, that's terrific honey. It's so nice to hear you interested in what I do."

I rolled my eyes, glad he couldn't see. Like this was something he actually did.

"So, can you get me access or what?"

"Sure. I'll call the head of security and get you cleared for a master card. Just give it a few minutes and go to the desk and make a new card, okay?"

"Thanks Dad. You can get back to whatever it was you were doing."

"I'm at a function, sweetie. Take care of yourself and I'll get back to New Orleans as soon as I can."

I waited a half-hour for good measure before heading down to the front desk. Adie was working and I noticed her eyeing me as I made the card.

"Is there a problem with your room key?" she asked suspiciously.

"Eh, no. I just need to be able to check something out for my dad," I muttered as I finished up. "Have a nice night," I called and waved as I walked away towards the elevator. Fortunately, the elevator was empty when it opened.

I inserted the key card, and pressed the basement button. This time it lit up. "Okay, that was easy," I said to myself as the elevator descended. Considering how easy it was to figure out, I started to feel silly for even bothering to snoop.

The elevator doors opened into pitch-blackness. I hadn't even considered bringing a flashlight. I reached for my phone in my back pocket. Using the illumination from the screen, I stepped out and heard the elevator doors slam closed behind me.

Barely able to see a foot ahead of me, I inched forward, reaching a hand out before me to brace myself. Before long, my palm hit onto to something hard and cold. I realized it was a door. Using the light from the phone to search for the handle, I yanked the door open, half expecting it to be locked. It wasn't, and light flooded through the doorway.

I felt the wings before I saw them, but it was the sight of so many black birds that made me jump. As the flapping died down, I moved through the doorway and turned around. Lanterns lit the interior space beyond the door and I watched five crows facing me from the side of the door I had just been on. Levi had told me they were originally crow shifters, but these birds in front of me seemed creepier than the Pterons. I wondered if Levi could communicate with the regular birds. I'd have to ask him. That is if I made it through my search of the basement first.

Letting the door close behind me, I tentatively stepped forward again, but I was distracted by the rich marble floors and walls around me. Detailed carvings that looked a lot like hieroglyphics were etched into the marble slab. In the dim light I made out a bunch of different animals, but most of the pictures were of birds.

I wrapped my arms around myself. Now that I could see, I realized just how cold it was. I walked down the corridor, a little spooked by the flickering lights of the lanterns. I noticed a number of doors ahead of me. Selecting the nearest one, I opened it, relieved that the lighting continued.

Entering the large circular room with rows of stone seating built into the side, I was struck most by carvings of two large birds on the marble floor. Rubies were inlaid in the pictures, giving the birds a majestic feel. I'd never seen gems used in flooring before, but it was gorgeous.

"It's beautiful, isn't it?"

I startled, turning around to face the source of the female voice.

"Natalie, umm hi," I stuttered.

"I'd ask you why you were down here, but really it was bound to happen with you dating Levi and all."

"You know Levi?"

She smiled. "Yes, I know Levi."

"Wait, so are you a—"

"Yes, I'm a Pteron. I had a feeling he let you in on the secret, but I wasn't sure."

"Wow. Umm, so I'm guessing this whole place down here has something to do with you, right? I mean all the bird stuff?"

"Of course."

"What's this room for?"

"For meetings. I really can't tell you more."

"Why not?"

123

"It's not my place. You should talk to Levi if you want answers."

"Why does it have to be him?"

She hesitated. "Because he's the one who's brought you in."

"Brought me in? You mean like in on the secret?"

"Yes, he must really think you're special." She smiled.

"I guess, but I don't know what makes me different from the rest of the girls he dates."

"The key word is dates. He has never really dated anyone seriously as far as I know. He's usually more of a one date kind of man."

"You mean he's a player?"

"That's one way of putting it."

I raised an eyebrow. "I know that, I'm not letting myself get too attached." I hoped my words were true.

"I'm not telling you that to scare you off. I'm letting you know he's been different with you, that's all."

I chose to press on with my own question, ignoring Natalie's implication. "Are you going to tell Levi I was down here?"

She looked towards the door suddenly. "I won't have to."

"What do you mean?"

"Doing some exploring?" Levi materialized through the doorway, walking towards us at a quick pace.

I tried to come up with an excuse but realized it was pointless. "All right, you got me."

"Natalie, can we have a minute?"

"Sure. I'll see you at work tomorrow morning?" she asked.

"Allie won't be at work tomorrow, we have plans." My mouth dropped open as I listened to him order her around. I waited for her rebuff. It never came.

"Of course. Goodnight."

I stared after her as she left, debating whether I should just follow. My curiosity got the better of me.

Levi closed the gap between us, standing directly in front of me. I couldn't help but shiver. I knew it was just Levi, but somehow he seemed a little scarier now that I was all alone with him in a room below ground that wasn't even supposed to exist. His next words did nothing to alleviate the growing unease.

"What am I going to do with you? You ever heard the saying 'curiosity killed the cat'?"

I said nothing, watching him carefully, repeating over and over to myself that the guy who kissed me so intensely the night before wasn't suddenly going to turn on me.

"I think I know what to do."

125

I tensed.

"Are you afraid?"

"Maybe." I said in barely a whisper. I shivered again.

He leaned towards me and I held in a breath. Confused and at a loss of what to do, I closed my eyes. I opened them seconds later when I felt his lips on mine. I pulled away, and he laughed.

"You were actually scared, weren't you?"

"Give me a break, Levi, it's creepy down here and I really know almost nothing about you. Of course you scared me."

"Well, you're not going to learn anything down here, let's go upstairs."

"At least tell me what this room is for."

"It's for meetings, Al. You happy?"

"Meetings? Is that really all you are going to give me?"

"Listen, I'd tell you more but then I'd have to kill you, and I already scared you enough for tonight."

"Levi!"

"Okay, okay. What do you want to know?"

"Everything. What is this? How do the Pterons fit in? Were you joking when you said there were actually vampires? What else is there—?"

"Whoa. Slow down there, babe. I can't answer them all at once."

"Well, you have to start somewhere."

"Does it have to be here? I can think of a few more comfortable places to discuss this."

"If this is another attempt to get into my room, forget it."

"Fine. This is the meeting room for *The Society*. The Pterons oversee it, but the council includes members from several different shifter groups. Lower lying groups like the vampires don't have seats."

"Vampires are low lying?"

"They suck blood from people, how much more of a bottom dweller can you imagine?"

"True. But I don't know... they seem more glamorous in books and movies."

"Yes, because books and movies always get things right." He shook his head.

"Fine. So why are the Pterons in charge?"

"We're the most powerful. Our hybrid form helps, as does our strength."

"So is your strength one of those abilities you promised to tell me about later?"

"Yes. Not that it should surprise you." He folded his arms across his chest, accentuating just how muscular he really was.

"No, I guess it isn't surprising." It was hard not to be impressed by his incredible physique. Even without knowing his secret, he appeared superhuman.

"If that about answers your questions, what do you say we get out of here?"

"This isn't over, but I'll take what I can get for tonight."

Levi walked me back to the elevator. He stayed behind, telling me he had a few things to do. I accepted his answers; glad I hadn't found anything more sinister. I reminded myself that this was just a summer fling—no reason to worry too much.

Eleven

Levi waited for me by the front entrance of the hotel the next morning. He grinned, and in the light of day I couldn't believe he had scared me the night before. I followed him outside to find his car. His black BMW matched him perfectly. It was such an obvious fit that I headed toward the passenger side door before he even told me it was his.

"How'd you know it was mine?"

"You said you were parked down here, and it seemed more you than an old Civic or a pickup."

He smiled and I could tell he was thinking. "I like how you don't hold back, Al. You just say it like it is."

"So you are really sticking to the Al thing, huh?"

"It fits."

"Whatever."

Taking the day off was a little too easy, and I felt bad about how quickly Natalie agreed when Levi asked. When I double-checked with her in the morning, she insisted I take the whole day and not worry about coming in that afternoon. I argued at first, but I could tell she wasn't going to budge. I had decided to stop worrying about it by the time I slipped into Levi's car, dressed as he suggested in jeans and sneakers.

"Are you ready to tell me where we're going?

"Patience, patience."

I yawned, tired from a fitful night of sleep. No matter how much I liked surprises, I couldn't deny the slight apprehension permeating my otherwise good mood.

Levi pulled up in front of a construction site. "Seriously? Do I seem like the type to like construction work?"

"No, but I think you'll like this." He smiled.

"Okay..." I stepped out of the car wondering where he was going with it.

A man in a hardhat greeted us as we walked closer to the house. "Levi, you made it."

"Hi, Phil. Of course. I brought another set of hands with me."

"I can see that."

"Allie, this is Phil. Phil, Allie."

"Nice to meet you," I said politely, taking his outstretched hand.

"The pleasure is all mine. We are always looking for new volunteers."

"Volunteers?" As the question slipped out, I looked around me, noticing for the first time that most of the people weren't your typical construction types.

"Yes. We've been doing rebuilding work since the storm, but it seems there is always more work to be done."

"I'm sure." Aware of the damage caused by Hurricane Katrina everything clicked. Levi had taken me to a rebuilding project.

"Do you know how to use a hammer?" Levi asked.

"I can't say I've ever used one, but I'm game to try."

***

Hours later with a tool belt slung around my hips and a hammer in my hands, I had successfully nailed together more boards than I could count. Sweaty and physically exhausted in a good way, I accepted the bottle of water Levi offered.

"Having fun?"

"Yeah, I actually am. It seems I have a hidden talent for hammering nails, huh?"

"It seems so." He laughed lightly, taking a swig from his own bottle. "We can head out if you want. I think Hailey wanted to steal you later."

"Steal me?"

"Absolutely, today was all mine, remember?"

"Do you do this a lot?" I asked.

"Usually once or twice a month. I did more right after Katrina, but I never really stopped."

"I'm glad you brought me."

"See, I'm not all bad."

"No, only 90%," I teased as we went to give back the tools.

"Ouch, this only buys me 10%?"

"What can I say, I have expensive taste."

"I'll keep that in mind."

***

Hailey was waiting for me in the lobby when Levi dropped me off. She followed me up to my room and flipped through some magazines while I showered and changed. "Did you have fun today?"

"Surprisingly, yes. I never would have thought construction would be my thing but it was fun, aside from the fact that my forearms are killing me. Honestly, I'm just shocked Levi does it."

"You know I'm not exactly a Levi cheerleader, but he's really not that bad, and no matter what you can say about him, he loves this city."

"Yeah, I get that sense."

"He'd do anything to help this place, and the city needs him."

"What do you mean?"

"I think that's for Levi to explain."

"Great, another opportunity for him to give me two word answers."

Hailey chuckled. "Yeah, he's pretty good at that, isn't he?"

"The best."

"You ready to go shopping?" she asked, replacing the magazines in the neat pile where I left them.

"Sure, but you never told me what was up with this impromptu shopping trip. Not that I need an excuse to shop."

132

"I wanted to hang out without the guys for once. There is only so much of my brother I can take."

I laughed. "Let me grab my bag."

***

Hailey drove us uptown in her red Jeep Cherokee. "Are you aware that your car matches your hair?" I asked as she wove her way through traffic.

"Ha ha, my hair is not that red."

"Okay, but it's close."

"If you're jealous, why don't we dye your hair purple like your car?"

"It's lavender and low blow. I didn't pick out the color." I regretted pointing my car out to her.

"Sure, sure. I thought we'd head up to Magazine Street. It's no Madison Avenue, but it's kind of fun and different," Hailey explained as she parallel parked along the street.

Hailey was right; Magazine Street was fun. Lined with a good mix of trendy and vintage boutiques, it kept us busy for several hours. Surprisingly, we didn't buy anything in the first few stores, but just as I was ready to congratulate myself on not spending any money, I found a dress I couldn't leave behind. Little, black, and a bit racy, I wasn't sure when I'd wear it, but it looked too good to resist.

"I might have to borrow that dress sometime," Hailey said as we waited for the clerk to put it in a garment bag.

"Deal, as long as I can borrow that skirt you picked out."

"Think of the clothing collection we'd have if we combined," Hailey laughed. Trying on clothes at the first store we had discovered we were the same size.

"Good point, maybe we can mail things back and forth."

"It's always nice to get packages." Hailey glanced down at her cell phone as we walked back to her car. "Wow, is it that late already?"

"Why? Do you have somewhere to be?"

"Kind of. I mean I can get out of it."

"What is it?"

"My soon to be roommate is in town for orientation and wants to meet up."

"Why aren't you at the orientation?" I asked.

"Oh, it's totally optional. I pretty much grew up on Tulane's campus so I don't need it. I tried to get out of meeting her, but she was pretty persistent."

"It might be nice to get to know her now instead of the awkward move-in meet and greet. I wish I could do that, I still don't know who my roommate is."

"If it's such a good idea, why don't you come with me?"

134

"Oh no, I'll take a cab back downtown or something."

"Please. I don't want to meet this girl by myself."

Hailey's discomfort at meeting her roommate surprised me so I questioned her on it, "Why not?"

"She just seems a little too bubbly to be safe."

"You do realize how ridiculous that sounds, right?"

"But I'm being totally serious. Something is off with her; no one is that perky naturally."

I laughed. "Where are you meeting her?"

"At PJ's. It's a coffee shop on campus. It could be fun; you haven't even seen the school yet."

"Sure, why not?" I shrugged before stowing my bag in the back of the jeep. I didn't have anywhere else to be, and I could tell that Hailey really wanted me to go.

We drove a few minutes before she parked along the curb. "We could never find a spot this close during the school year, but it's fairly quiet on campus over the summer."

"Yeah, it looks that way." I glanced around the street lined with dorms, and one open grassy area. I'd always loved college campuses, and being on one reminded me that I was really going to be a college student in a few months.

I followed Hailey into a coffee shop located on the first floor of a brick dorm. Glancing around, I noticed that a scattering of tables were taken, and I figured many of the students were pre-frosh in town for orientation. "Do you know what your roommate looks like?"

"Yeah, black hair and—"

"Hailey! Hi!" A petite girl hugged a startled Hailey. "It is so nice to finally meet you!"

"Umm, hi Anne. It's nice to meet you, too." Hailey gave me an "omg" look over Anne's head. "You look just like your picture on Facebook."

"So do you!" Anne said with a lot of enthusiasm.

"Oh, hi there. I'm Anne. Are you going to be a freshman too?" She reached out to shake my hand. I guess I wasn't entitled to the hug treatment.

"Hi, I'm Allie and I'll be a freshman, but not here."

"Oh, where are you going?"

"Princeton."

"Cool. Are you from New Orleans then?" she asked.

"No. I'm just here for the summer."

"Fun! I found us a table already." Following her gaze, I noticed a table with a large to-go cup on it.

"Why don't you go ahead Hailey? I'm going to get a chai tea, you want anything?"

"Make that two."

"Okay, see you in a sec."

With our teas in hand, I joined Hailey and Anne. Passing Hailey's cup over, I tried not to interrupt their conversation.

"It's awesome you're from here. That means you know all the best places to go out, right? My dad wanted me to stay closer to home in Jackson, but there was no way I was giving up the chance to go to school in New Orleans."

"Yeah, definitely," Hailey said unenthusiastically.

"Have you decided what classes you are taking yet? I'm pre-med so I have to take Chemistry and I want to get my freshman writing over with, but otherwise I have no clue," Anne said all in one breath. The girl could talk fast.

"I'm going to be an art history major, so I need to get into the intro class, and I'll probably take French as well," Hailey answered.

"And you Allie? Have you picked your classes yet?"

"Not yet, but I'm majoring in business."

"Business? You so don't seem like a business major," Hailey said.

"Yeah, I'd probably major in biology if it were up to me, but my dad wouldn't go for that."

"Wow, it sounds like your dad is as controlling as mine," Anne said sympathetically before changing the subject again with no warning. "So Hailey, you must know *tons* of people here? Know any cute guys to introduce me to?"

"Not really, sorry." I had never seen Hailey so uncomfortable.

"Speaking of guys, we need to have a system of letting each other know when we have male company."

"Excuse me?" Hailey nearly spit out the first sip of her tea. "You do know we're in JL, one of the girl's dorms, right?"

"Of course I know that, but I've asked around and there are ways to get around the check in rules."

"I really don't think we need to worry about that now."

"I just think we should have a signal. Socks on the door handle seem too cliché, how about we use panties?"

Hailey and I froze looking at each other in disbelief.

"Just kidding." Anne giggled.

I really wasn't sure she was.

Aside from the look of panic on Hailey's face as Anne described her panty suggestion, the evening was fairly enjoyable. Anne was pretty intense, but I could tell she was nice and Hailey could do worse in a roommate. Watching their somewhat awkward conversation reminded me of what I faced arriving at Princeton at the end of the summer. Not only did I have to meet a new roommate, I also had to face Toby. By the time our acceptances had rolled in I was already starting to doubt the permanency of our relationship. College was about a fresh start, now I had to start with an ex-boyfriend.

"Allie?" Hailey called me back from spacing out.

"Oh sorry, what were you saying?"

"I was telling Anne how you had to get home early…"

"Oh yeah, sorry, but it was really nice to meet you," I said with a smile.

"Same here! You'll have to come down for a visit this year. Maybe for Mardi Gras?"

"Sure, that could be fun." As I agreed, I imagined visiting Levi and discovered I didn't mind that thought at all.

Hailey grabbed my arm as we hurried down the brick steps of the outdoor patio. "Oh my god. Oh my god. Did she seriously suggest putting panties on our door?"

I snickered. "Yeah, I believe she did."

"Shoot me. Who says something like that?"

"Aw, she seemed nice, maybe a little too over eager."

"Nice? Let's try scary."

"Calm down, Hailey. She's just your roommate, you don't have to be best friends."

"Great, now you sound like my mom."

"I'm only trying to help," I said defensively. I wasn't used to this side of Hailey. My gut reaction would have been to snap back at her, but I figured she was just really nervous about starting college and I knew the feeling.

"I know and I appreciate it. Are you in a rush to get home?" She calmed down.

"Not really, why?"

"Are you up for some ice cream?"

"Sure, I'm always up for ice cream." I smiled

Twenty minutes later we were enjoying waffle cones filled with decadent vanilla Häagen-Dazs. Unable to find a seat inside, we took our cones outside, dripping sticky ice cream with sprinkles all over us as it melted.

After finishing our cones, we headed back to the car. The main lot of the shopping center had been full, so we'd parked on a side street a little ways down. It was dark out, and I was ready to get back to the car and the hotel.

"You do realize our dinner tonight consisted of a chai tea and ice cream, right?" I laughed.

"Yeah, that's why we went for the extra scoop." She smiled. "Thanks again for coming with me. I know I was pretty bitchy back there."

"It's okay, and this was a good way to make up for it. Anyway, thanks for treating."

"No problem—Hey! What the hell are you doing?" Hailey sprinted the remaining distance to her car.

A man was trying unsuccessfully to break into the driver's side of the jeep. Whipping around, he took out a gun and pointed it at us. "Get back and drop your bags."

"Get away from my car," Hailey demanded without a sign of backing down.

"Let's just give him our stuff. I'd rather not die right now." I barely choked the words out. My flight response was ready to take over.

"Not a chance," she fumed.

"I told you to back up, bitch," the man yelled.

Without warning Hailey moved like a blur and had the guy's arm pinned behind him and slammed on the hood of the jeep. "You had better not have scratched my car!" She tossed him like he weighed nothing. Her eyes were completely black. Picking up the gun from where it flew during their altercation, she calmly pulled out the clip before throwing the rest of the gun into the bushes.

"Open the back and pull out some rope," she directed.

"Rope?" I asked as I walked around the car. Sure enough, there was a length of rope.

I tossed it to Hailey who proceeded to tie the guy to a tree.

"You just happen to have rope in your car?"

"It's climbing rope. I occasionally climb and you never know when you're going to need it," she explained.

"What kind of freak are you?" The guy started coming around.

Hailey kicked him in the stomach shutting him up. "Let's get out of here."

Hesitantly, I opened the passenger door and slipped inside. Hailey joined me with a quick glance over her shoulder. "He scratched my door. I shouldn't have been so nice."

"You can't seriously be worrying about your door right now! Shouldn't we call the police?"

"No, how would we explain what just happened? The scumbag would talk. I'll have to call the cleanup guy."

I sat silently as she placed her call. "Gary, it's me. I had a slight mishap off Carrolton tonight. I kind of left a guy incapacitated." She laughed. "He was trying to steal my car, but I took care of it. All right, thanks."

"We're set." Hailey pulled out and we headed back downtown. She watched the road like nothing had even happened.

"Any chance you can teach me how to fight like that?" I knew I was in shock, because the fact that a guy had held a gun on us hadn't quite set in yet. My mind could however, handle Hailey's awesome moves.

"No, it's not really something I can teach."

"You're incredible."

"Tell my brother and his friends that. I'm the resident weakling. Wait until you see the others in action."

I could only imagine what Levi must be like.

Hailey dropped me off out front of the hotel.

"Thanks for an, um, interesting night," I said, opening my door before grabbing my bag from the back.

She laughed. "I'm glad you still have a sense of humor. I'll see you soon."

"Night!"

The reality of the danger we'd been in finally hit me as I entered my room. I checked the locks on my door and balcony twice before getting ready for bed.

My heart nearly jumped out of my chest when I heard a faint knock on the balcony door. After a moment, I realized that no one trying to break in would knock. I tentatively pulled back the curtains to reveal Levi, wearing a white tank that must have allowed room for his wings. Opening the door, I wordlessly ushered him in.

"What are you doing here?" I snapped, well aware that my cami and shorts pjs left little to the imagination. Levi seemed to realize it too because it took him a moment to respond.

"I heard what happened and wanted to make sure you were okay."

"I'm fine." I certainly wasn't about to admit that I was glad for his presence, but I decided to take the attitude down a notch. "But it was thoughtful of you to come."

"Well, I'm glad you decided to let me in tonight, last time you practically slammed the door in my face." He grinned.

"I guess tonight's your lucky night." The second the words left my mouth I regretted them, especially as I watched his eyes widen. "Um, scratch that. Not lucky in that way."

Figuring that honesty was probably the only way I was getting my proverbial foot out of my mouth, I admitted to my fear. "Fine, I'm glad you're here. Tonight was pretty scary. I mean Hailey took care of the situation quickly but I've never had someone pull a gun on me before." Admitting it out loud made it more real and I started to shake.

"It's okay. I promise that guy has been taken care of."

"What do you mean?" I wasn't sure that I wanted to hear the answer.

"He's been apprehended. Leave it at that."

"Okay…"

"Come here." Levi sat down on the couch, opening his arms up to me. Without hesitating I snuggled into him, leaning my head on his chest. His warm skin felt good against mine as he gently kissed the top of my head.

"It's normal to be scared. Not everyone is like Hailey and can just let something like that slide. Don't fight it."

I didn't say anything; I just let him hold me.

"Do you want me to stay?" he asked quietly.

I wanted to take him up on it, but my pride wouldn't let me. "No, I'll be fine."

"If it makes you feel any better, this hotel is probably the safest place in the city." He didn't press his offer further and I appreciated it.

"Oh." Remembering the secret rooms beneath the hotel, I figured that security was probably pretty good. "It does make me feel better." I picked my head up from his chest, and smiled to let him know I was okay.

"Call me if you need anything or you just want to talk." He stood up and walked toward the balcony door before pausing. "Thanks, by the way." He grinned sheepishly and I was afraid to take the bait.

"For?"

"The image. I was wondering what you slept in. Goodnight, Al." As usual, he suddenly took off before I could respond. I didn't mind his comment, he had been attempting to lighten the mood and it worked.

"Goodnight, Levi," I whispered even though I knew he couldn't hear me.

Twelve

"What kind of party are we going to?" I asked while slipping into the passenger seat of Hailey's jeep. When she called me during work to see if I was free, I thought it was to hang out like usual. I wasn't expecting a party, especially not one that came with warnings.

"Well, you might be the only human there, but I guess there could be a few others."

"Lovely. You do realize how weird it is when you say things like that, right?"

She laughed. "Uh-huh, but you'll get used to it. Just be careful who you talk to, and don't go off alone with anyone, okay?"

"Really? Because I was planning on going home with some random guy tonight."

"Seriously, Allie, these guys aren't the type to mess around with. Not to mention I'd have my head served up on a platter if you did that."

"You do realize I was joking, right?"

"Yeah, but I just wanted to emphasize how important it is that you're careful."

"If it's so dangerous, then why are we going?"

"Because it's going to be a good party, and I know for a fact my brother and his friends won't be there."

"Okay, good enough reasons."

146

"I'm glad, because I wasn't going to turn around even if you didn't like them." She gave me a cheeky grin.

Something about Hailey's expression reminded me of Owen, so I decided to ask a question that I'd been mulling over for a while. "Can I ask you something about your brother?"

"My brother? Sure…"

"Why is he single? I mean I haven't seen him even flirt with anyone."

"So you noticed? Yeah, he got hurt pretty badly and hasn't dated since. I think he's too scared of being that vulnerable again."

"Why, what happened?" I asked, my curiosity getting the better of me.

"He met a girl freshman year, Chloe. They got pretty serious, and he planned to propose to her."

"He wanted to get engaged at what, 19 years old?"

"Yeah, I know, pretty young. But anyway, he knew before he could ask her he had to tell her the truth about who we are, and well, let's just say she didn't take things as well as you did."

"She broke up with him when she found out he was a Pteron?" It's not that I could blame her, it was shocking, but at least for me it was also incredibly cool.

"She did more than that. She transferred schools, changed her number and everything."

"Oh, geez."

"Yeah, he was crushed and never really got over it. I think he was worried you would do the same thing to Levi."

"Oh… So I understand him not wanting to be with another human, but why not date a Pteron? Wouldn't that solve the problem?"

"Uh, we're not exactly encouraged to date our own. Plus, there aren't too many girls."

"Why aren't you supposed to date each other?"

She peeked over hesitantly. "Well, dating would be fine, but we aren't supposed to get serious and Owen wants serious. But anyway, it's about keeping some variation in the gene pool. It's supposed to keep us stronger. The Pteron gene is 100% dominant so as long as one partner is a Pteron, your kids will be."

"Oh. Great." I wasn't sure what to make of the genetics talk, but I appreciated Hailey being open with me.

"So why doesn't he just date other shifters then?"

Hailey laughed dryly. "That's seen as the worse affront possible."

"Wait, so you are encouraged to date humans but not other shifters?"

"Yeah. It's considered dating down. Humans are like a blank slate, whereas other supernaturals are considered tainted. Don't ask."

"Okay…" I decided not to press further and tried to steer us back to a safer topic. "So where are we going exactly?" I looked down at my tank and short jean skirt, glad that Hailey was dressed similarly. I wasn't quite sure what to wear to a shifter party.

"It's at a warehouse on Tchoupitoulas street."

"Say that again."

Hailey laughed. "Chop-a-too-lus." She exaggerated the phonetic syllables of the word. "Try saying that five times fast."

I smiled. "No thanks. I've never been to a warehouse party before, but then again I've never been to a party with shifters either, so I guess the location is the less important part."

"It should be fun. These things are usually pretty entertaining."

"Who's throwing this party anyway?"

Hailey parked. "Just a couple of Weres I know."

"Weres? Wait, like werewolves?"

"Yeah. And just follow my lead." Hailey got out of the car, slamming her door behind her. I hopped out and we walked up towards a large abandoned building. I didn't say anything, but the whole thing had me a little nervous.

Hailey led us to a doorway and I stopped short when I noticed two large guys standing on either side like bouncers.

"Code," one boomed while simultaneously checking us out. The other guy didn't even acknowledge us.

149

"Howling wolf," Hailey said evenly. If I wasn't so nervous the password would have made me laugh.

"Head on up."

"Come on." She grabbed my hand and we moved inside and into an industrial elevator. Pulling the grate down, she gave me an encouraging grin. "Let's do this."

I could feel the beat of the music as Hailey pulled up the grate when the elevator reached the top floor. We took a short flight of stairs to the roof. We could now hear, as well as feel, the loud dance music as we stepped out. Strands of lights illuminated the roof, giving it a warm feel I wasn't expecting. After a quick glance at each other, we moved into the crowd of dancers.

We danced with each other for a while, laughing as a few guys made a ridiculous attempt at break dancing.

"All right, I need a rest," Hailey said after several songs, walking away from the crowd. I followed; glad I had decided to come with her. There was something fun about going to a party where you knew no one. So much less pressure and work.

"Hailey?" A couple of guys headed toward us.

"Hey, Jason." Hailey smiled at a guy around our age with light brown hair.

"I didn't expect to see you here." He stuffed his hands into the pockets of his jeans.

"Yeah, there wasn't much else going on," she said nonchalantly. "This is my friend, Allie."

"Hey, Allie, nice to meet you." Jason reached out his hand, but it was quickly pushed away by his friend.

"Hi Allie, I'm C.J. Welcome to our party. I don't think I've ever seen you around before." With spiky black hair, a sports coat and a pair of Chuck Taylors, C.J. was like a walking contradiction. I had a feeling he thought it was part of his charm.

"She's from New York," Hailey interrupted.

"Ah, trading up are you?" C.J. asked. I wasn't sure what he was asking, so I looked over at Hailey for help and she nodded.

"Yeah, I needed a change."

"I get it. You wanted to check out some new stomping grounds, or I guess skies." He gave me a flirtatious smile and it hit me; he thought I was a Pteron. I smiled back at him, pretty happy about his assumption. It wasn't a bad thing if guys thought you were super-strong and able to fly.

"Want to dance?" C.J. asked, gesturing to the swelling crowd.

"Umm, I think I'm going to get a drink," I replied, trying not to hurt the guy's ego, but I wasn't interested.

"All right, let's get some drinks then." He reached to grab my arm and I stepped away. If he had been a regular guy I would have made my feelings clear, but the knowledge that he was actually a werewolf made me rein in my temper.

"Great. Hailey, you want to come?"

Half expecting Hailey to pull a Jess and ditch me for the guy she was talking to, I was pleasantly surprised by her response. "Definitely, we do *everything* together."

Trying to make sure he understood Hailey's implication, C.J. just stared after us as we slipped away arm in arm.

"Nice one." I laughed.

"Yeah, he seemed like a clinger."

"So, can they really not tell?" I asked, hoping she got what I was actually asking.

"Nope. You can only sense a Pteron when we shift."

"Oh. I guess I was thinking there was a scent or something."

"A scent? Nope, I mean what would a crow smell like?"

I shrugged. "I don't know, a bird?"

Hailey laughed.

After grabbing some drinks, we decided to dance again, and I groaned inwardly when C.J. and Jason caught up with us. I didn't push to lose them again because Hailey seemed to like Jason enough, but I wasn't so gentle removing C.J.'s hands from my waist the second time.

"Feisty one, huh?" he whispered in my ear and I cringed.

Ready with a comeback, I was startled as two arms wrapped around my body possessively.

"Put your damn paws on her again and you'll be short one," Levi growled from just above my shoulder.

"Oh, hi Levi. I didn't realize you hadn't had this one yet. What do you care anyway, don't you usually go for the humans?"

Levi's arms released me and he pushed me behind him, placing me right between Jared and Owen.

"Humans are superior to you lowlifes," Levi spat.

"You have the nerve to come to my party and insult me?"

"I can insult you anywhere I want, *dog*."

I glanced over at Hailey, noticing that her eyes had gone all black again. Jared and Owen's had as well, and I could only assume Levi's had done the same. Before I could dwell on it too long, I watched with shock as the air seemed to buzz and C.J. shifted into a giant wolf. Unlike the transformation of the Pterons, C.J. became a wolf completely; there was nothing human about him.

Levi's wings flapped out behind him, as did Jared and Owen's. The sheer size of the wings, and the black eyes made for a menacing sight.

"Stay with Allie and don't move," Levi yelled at Hailey. She nodded, leading us back to lean against a wall. I followed her lead shakily.

Several other girls and guys transformed into wolves, and I had to steady myself against the wall from the craziness of it all.

153

A snarl emanated from the wolf that was C.J. Levi strode up to the wolf, picked him up by the scruff of his neck and tossed him. "Anyone else going to dare to disrespect me?" Levi screamed, hands balled into fists. "You do not touch our women. Do you understand?"

No one said anything.

"Let's go!" Levi pulled me to his side and away from Hailey. With his arms around my waist, he jumped off the building.

Releasing me as soon as we reached the ground, Levi spun on Hailey angrily. "What the hell were you thinking? A Were party? What, you slumming it now? And you thought it was acceptable to take Allie with you? Are you dense?"

I expected Owen to tell Levi to back off, but instead he looked at Hailey with the same steely gaze. The fury coming from all three of the guys was terrifying, and it wasn't even directed at me.

Hailey didn't falter. "We were having fun until you showed up."

"And what would you have done if that punk tried to push things further with Allie?"

"I would have protected her. I can take care of myself and her."

"What, now that you have your full strength you think you're invincible?" Levi seethed.

"Get real, Hailey. You might be stronger than a Were but there is nothing you could have done against a whole party of those guys." Jared entered the lecture.

I knew it was time to jump in. "Stop it! Stop yelling at her. I decided to come with her, so it's my fault too."

"It's not your fault, but I do wish you had bothered to tell me where you were going." Levi wrung his hands, looking like he wasn't sure how much he should say to me.

"Since when do I have to check in with you every time I go out?"

"Since you decided to spend time with Weres. You have no idea how dangerous they can be."

"Not as dangerous as you."

"The difference is I'm not going to hurt you. They would."

I wanted to keep arguing but I sensed he was right. C.J. hadn't actually hurt me, but even with his strange style, I knew he was a lot stronger than me, and I wouldn't last long trying to fight him.

"Can we just go home?" I pleaded. Hailey now looked completely defeated and I wanted the night to end.

"Of course, I'll take you home," Levi said immediately.

"Flying?"

"I have my car."

"Is that okay, Hailey?"

"It's fine." She waved me on.

As Levi snaked his arm around my waist and led me away, I heard Owen continuing to lecture his sister. "You can't talk to him like that! You have to

155

respect him. Mom and Dad would kill you if they heard you talking that way."

My hunch that Levi was something important to the Pterons was fast becoming impossible to deny, and I was completely prepared to broach the topic with him when he pulled me into a near bone-crunching hug.

"Are you all right? I didn't think to ask before."

"I'm fine. I have a lot of questions, but I'm fine."

"Can the questions wait?" he asked.

"For tonight, but you can't put them off forever."

"Are you sure about that?"

"Completely."

Levi opened the passenger door for me and I slipped inside. He closed my door before walking around to get in.

I turned to him as he pulled away from the curb. "Okay, can I at least ask one question?"

He nodded. "I don't have a choice, do I?"

"How'd you know where we were?"

"Why, are you worried I'm following you now?"

"Not exactly, I just need to know." He wasn't completely off. As the shock of the transformations wore off, I realized that there was no reason for Levi to have known where we were.

"It's nothing that dramatic. Hailey left the email about the party open on her computer. Her mom found it and called Owen to get her."

"Oh..." I said.

"So no more questions for tonight then?"

"Could I ask one more?"

He glanced over at me as we sat at a red light. He held my hand in my lap. "You're a hard girl to say no to."

"Who are you, Levi? What is it that you're not telling me?"

He turned away but didn't drop my hand. "No more questions. It's late and I need to get you home."

I could tell by the way that he watched the road with unwavering attention that he wasn't going to answer my question. I also realized that his unwillingness to answer was just as telling as any explanation he would have given.

Thirteen

Despite the fact that I was dating a guy with wings and superhuman powers, things eventually settled down into a routine. Between work all day and spending my nights with Levi and Hailey, the time went by far too quickly. The one thing we never talked about was the Were party. Everyone else acted like it never happened. Hailey seemed to be getting along with the guys again, and I was afraid to ruin things by bringing it up.

I talked to Jess a few times, but not nearly as much as we usually would. It's not that it was that awkward, but it felt like we were in different worlds for the first time ever. I hoped she didn't secretly blame me for what happened with Jared. We had one ridiculous game of phone tag that lasted two weeks. I was relieved when we finally broke it.

She must have been holding her phone because she picked up on the first ring. "Hey, we finally made contact."

"Does that win for longest game of phone tag ever?" I laughed.

"Maybe. But how are you? Are things going well with Levi?"

"Yeah, they really are. I've discovered there's a lot more to him than I thought." I smiled to myself realizing just how true that statement was.

"I told you so."

"Yeah, well, I have no idea where it's going to go, but it's fun."

"Sure. You can't have changed that much, Allie, but I don't have time to argue, I actually have to run." I could tell she had put me on speakerphone and was moving around her room.

"Any place interesting?"

"Emmett's coming over. We're giving it another try." I could almost hear her smiling through the phone.

"That's awesome, good for you. I always thought you guys were great together."

She laughed. "I know, you had a harder time with us breaking up than I did."

"I'm really happy for you, Jess."

"Thanks! And he's going to Fordham so we'll be able to see each other all the time even when school starts. He says we'll have to make next year a re-do of the senior year we never had together."

"Ha ha, good plan."

"All right, so I'm glad we talked, call me when you get back in town." She rushed to end the call.

"Definitely. Tell Emmett I said hi."

"Same to Levi."

"Okay, bye."

I sighed with relief as soon as I hung up. It sounded like Jess was doing okay. Something still felt weird with us, but I hoped when I saw her again things would get back to normal.

***

One of the perks of staying at the hotel was that we got to use the pool. I learned pretty early on that a pool was a hot commodity with such intense heat in New Orleans. Hailey and I spent a lot of time laying out on my days off.

"Can you believe it's August?" Hailey asked as we lounged by the pool.

"Not at all. This summer has flown by."

"Are you ready?" She didn't say what for, but I knew she meant college.

"I guess so, but I'm nervous too. I just want it to be great. You know? Your freshman year of college is supposed to be incredible and I'm scared it's just going to be some major letdown. What if I mess up my classes, or Toby doesn't leave me alone, or I have horrible girls on my floor?" Once I started, the worries just spilled out.

"So I'm not the only one? I can't tell you how good it is to hear you have the same fears. Well, aside from the Toby part." She laughed.

I smiled lightly and thought about the one worry I had left out—Levi. Things with him were heating up and I wasn't sure I wanted to say goodbye at the end of the summer. Trying to quell thoughts of a long distance relationship, I reminded myself that he probably had no interest in one, and besides who wanted to start college in a relationship?

"If it makes you feel any better, he doesn't want you to leave either," Hailey said as she lathered on some more sunscreen. Her pale skin burned easily, and she was ultra-careful in the sun.

"How'd you know I was thinking about him?"

"You always get that the same look when he's on your mind."

"What look?"

"The love-struck one." She saw my face and backtracked. "Okay, well the far off one."

"Do you really think he cares that I'm leaving?"

"Umm yeah. He even—" She stopped herself.

"What? He even what?"

"I really don't want to get myself in any more trouble. Levi is already annoyed at me."

"Please, you have to tell me. I won't tell."

"Fine," she said dramatically but I sensed she wanted to say it anyway. "I heard him talking to my brother about whether he could handle something long-distance."

"He what?" That was the last thing I expected to hear, and I didn't know how I felt about it. On the one hand, it terrified me that there could be something real between us, but on the other hand, the same thought thrilled me. This was not what I needed.

"I'm sure he wasn't really serious about it. We've known from the start whatever this is between us is just for fun."

"Whatever you say." Hailey smiled but dropped it. I loved how she always knew where to draw the line.

I woke up to a knock on the door at 10:30 that night. I'd fallen asleep on the couch watching a dumb reality TV show. Hailey had some sort of family obligation and Levi had a meeting with his dad, so I had settled in front of the TV after taking advantage of time to myself to finalize my class schedule.

"Who is it?" I called, expecting Levi or Hailey to answer.

"It's me, honey."

"Mom?" I asked as I threw open the door.

We nearly knocked one another over pulling each other into a huge hug. She rolled a bag into the room. "I heard you had an extra room. Your dad tried to talk me into taking my own, but I figured this would be more fun."

"Good! But what are you doing here?"

"Does a mother really need an excuse to visit her daughter?"

"Come on, Mom."

"Okay, you sounded distant the last time we talked and I'd thought I'd check in."

I sensed there was more to her visit than she let on, but I didn't press. "Well, I'm glad you're here, whatever the reason. I was thinking about making popcorn, you want some?"

"Definitely." Mom strolled around the suite while I waited for the popcorn to finish. "Nice place your dad set you up in."

"Yeah. It's a little large for just me, but the space was nice when Jess was here."

"Have you talked to her?"

"We've talked a few times, but it feels off, like we're only chatting superficially."

We took a seat on the couch, munching popcorn.

"Now that we're face to face, do you want to tell me what really happened?"

"What do you mean?"

She gave me a sympathetic look. "I know she didn't leave because she was homesick."

"It was because of a guy," I admitted.

"I gathered that much. It's Jess we're talking about."

"She made a mistake with a guy and I think it scared her."

"All right, I get the idea."

"It threw her for a loop, and she just needed to leave. I also think it made her miss Emmett. I should have been looking out for her, but she always acts so tough about boys that I didn't think I needed to protect her."

"It's not your fault, and she knows it. Just give her time."

"I know. I just don't want it to change our friendship."

"Whether this thing with the boy happened or not, your friendship was going to change. You're

163

both going to college. You'll have different groups of friends and activities."

"So you're saying we're going to drift apart anyway?"

"No. I'm just saying that your friendship will change—good or bad. It's inevitable."

I sighed.

"It's just part of growing up, but I can take a hint. Enough of that topic and onto another awkward one."

"Yeah?"

"Toby came by the house last week." Mom pursed her lips; I could tell she was hesitant to broach the subject.

"What?"

"He says you aren't returning his calls and that some guy answered once."

"Oh."

"So who's the guy?"

"Oh, just a friend, no big deal."

"You sure?" Mom studied me skeptically.

"Yeah, nothing to worry about."

"Do you think you're going to give Toby another chance?"

"No. It's over between us." I crossed my arms, Mom and I had already discussed this enough, and it annoyed me that he brought her into it again.

"You sure about that? He seems to think otherwise."

"I'm sure."

A loud knock on the door interrupted us and my stomach dropped as I realized it was probably Levi.

Hesitating a moment too long, my mom got up to open the door. "Well, hello there."

"Oh, hi. Is Allie around?" Levi poked his head out, as if to double check the room number.

I got up and walked over to the doorway. "Hey."

"Hey." He looked at me questioningly.

"Aren't you going to introduce us, sweetie?"

"Oh yeah, Mom this is Levi."

"It's so nice to meet you Ms.—" Levi held out his hand at a loss for my mother's last name.

"It's O'Connor but call me Diane."

"Well it's nice to meet you, Diane. I've heard a lot about you."

"Have you? Funny, I haven't heard anything about you. Unless, is this the friend I didn't need to concern myself with?" I was busted. Mom didn't get annoyed easily but keeping stuff from her was a sure way to set her off.

For the first time in recent memory I was at a loss for words.

"Well, I'll let you enjoy your time with your mother. Call me sometime. Once again, nice to meet you."

"Wait, Levi. Do you have plans tomorrow night? We would love to have you join us for dinner. Allie's father will be there as well."

Please say no, please say no, I repeated over and over waiting for his response. "I would love to join you for dinner. What time were you thinking?"

"Around seven o'clock down in the lobby?"

"Perfect, I look forward to it. Good night, Allie." Levi wore an unreadable expression as he walked out the door, and for once, I wished he had called me Al.

As soon as the door closed, Mom turned to me. "So yes, I agree, Toby has no chance."

"Mom!"

"What? I'm not blind. Toby has no chance against him, especially not with the way he was looking at you."

"Mom, it's really not a big deal."

"I'll be the judge of that."

I groaned. "Please, can we just drop it for tonight?"

"Sure, I'll get my answers tomorrow. Besides, I can't really be that mad at you."

"What do you mean?"

"I've been keeping a bit of a secret myself."

My stomach dropped again. "What kind of secret?"

"I'm seeing someone new."

"Oh? Anyone I know?"

"You know his son."

"Who?" I asked with trepidation.

"Andrew Thomas."

"What? You know how much I hate Andrew."

"Yes, but that doesn't change the fact that I like his dad. Besides, maybe you shouldn't be so hard on Andrew. He thought you made the right decision to dump Toby."

"Of course he did! He's been trying to sleep with me since the 8th grade!"

"Allie, stop it."

"It's true! The kid is a total perv and seriously can't take a hint."

"Well, you're going to have to get over your differences when you get home in a few weeks. You're not going to ruin this for me."

I regretted my reaction immediately. The look of disappointment on her face hurt. "Of course not. I'm sorry. It just surprised me."

"Yeah, I know how that feels."

"I'm sorry," I said guiltily.

"So, are you ready to call it a night?"

"Yeah. I'm glad you're here Mom."

"Me too," she said as we hugged.

Lying in bed, I worried about whether Levi was mad that I hadn't mentioned him to Mom. I contemplated calling him but stopped myself each time. I'd face him soon enough anyway.

***

167

After a day of sightseeing and catching up with Mom, I was almost ready for dinner. Dad was finally back in town, and I was sure the timing was anything but coincidental. He wasn't about to let Mom think he was inattentive. She always gave him a hard time about not taking enough of an interest in me. I told her I didn't care, but she assured me I would care one day. Dad met up with us in my room before we headed down to the lobby.

Levi glanced up from his phone as we approached. Wearing one of his usual Lacoste shirts, he had exchanged his jeans for a pair of khaki slacks. He looked like he had walked off a magazine shoot as he gave me another look I couldn't quite read.

Levi didn't miss a beat. "Hi Allie, Diane. Mr. Davis, it's nice to finally meet you. I'm Levi."

Dad shook his hand. "Hello, Levi, please call me Tim."

"All right, Tim."

"So you're the one my little girl has been spending all her time with?"

My mom glared at me and I shrugged. I had no idea how Dad knew about him.

"Yes, I have been monopolizing her attention all summer. I just can't seem to get enough of her." Levi smiled and he seemed much more relaxed suddenly.

"Allie told you about Levi?" Mom asked.

Arrgh. I could see where this was going.

"She didn't have to tell me. I know what's going on in my daughter's life. I'm sorry she didn't feel the need to share it with you."

"She didn't actually tell you then?"

"Not exactly," Dad said through clenched teeth.

"So how did you hear?"

"Oy vey, Diane. You got me. No one actually told me, I only assumed."

"Just like I thought." Mom smiled smugly.

I glanced at Levi whose mouth was pressed in a firm line again.

"Okay, let's get to dinner before someone gets killed," I said quickly.

"Good idea." Levi put his arm around me as we headed to the front entrance. He leaned in to whisper in my ear. "Is this okay, *friend?*"

"Please don't start," I pleaded quietly. Dinner might be worse than I thought.

"Oh, I haven't gotten started yet, babe."

"Lovely."

We were given a corner table at the Palace Café. I was seated between Levi and my father, and my mother sat directly across from me. The way she smiled at me as we perused the menu let me know she was also gearing up.

Thankfully, things stayed calm long enough for Dad to order wine.

"So Levi, are you in school or have you graduated?"

"I'm about to start my senior year at Tulane."

"Any plans yet for after graduation?" Dad asked.

"Dad, you don't need to interrogate him."

"It's fine. I don't mind in the slightest. I'm going to be working in the family business," Levi explained.

"And what kind of business is that?" Dad asked with obvious interest.

"It's a large diversified corporation; we've got hands in a lot of places."

"Sounds a lot like my own. What did you say the name was?"

"I didn't. It's the Laurent Corporation."

"Oh wow, I had no idea."

Levi smiled politely.

"Will your business keep you in New Orleans, Levi? Any plans to spend time in the Northeast after graduation?"

"We're very locally based, but there are some travel opportunities if I'm inclined."

"I see." Mom smiled lightly.

The waiter brought over the wine and we ordered dinner. I hoped the conversation would lighten up.

"How did you two meet?"

I deliberated how to answer, but Levi didn't give me a chance. "Your daughter first caught my eye in the lobby of the hotel, but I didn't have the

170

pleasure of meeting her formally until I ran into her at a karaoke bar of all places."

"A karaoke bar?" Mom said with surprise.

"Yes. Allie and her friend did a lovely rendition of *Girls Just Want to Have Fun*."

"I was wondering about that. Why isn't Jessica joining us tonight?" Dad asked.

Mom's face turned to stone. "Do you mean to tell me you weren't aware that Jess left weeks ago? You had no idea of this when you left our daughter alone in a hotel suite on Bourbon Street of all places and with Casanova over there?" Mom pointed to Levi who smirked.

I spared my dad from answering. "Mom, I'm starting college in the fall, I don't need to be babysat."

"Princeton is not New Orleans."

"No it's not, but it's still unsupervised. Besides, I could have come to college in New Orleans if I wanted."

Levi looked at me with interest.

"But you're not. Your father shouldn't have left you."

"What's done is done, it's not an issue. Now please can we enjoy the evening?" As if on cue, our meals arrived and I sighed with relief.

"So where do you live, Levi? Are you on campus?" Dad asked, trying to put someone else on the hot seat.

"I only lived on campus one year. I live in an apartment with a few friends. It's a nice place. Isn't it, Allie?"

I kicked him under the table, what was he playing at?

"Oh, Allie has seen it?" Mom asked.

"Yes, she's spent plenty of evenings there."

I was going to kill him. "Evenings meaning hanging out. The only time I stayed over was on the couch. Okay? Can we please change the subject?"

"Of course." Levi smirked again. "So Diane, how long are you in town for?"

"I leave tomorrow morning. I only wanted to check in on Allie since no one else apparently is."

"Oh, that's too bad. I would have loved to introduce you to my parents."

"What?" I was sure my mouth was hanging open.

"How thoughtful, that would have been nice."

"My parents know all about Allie and are so excited to meet her." Levi challenged me with his stare.

"It's nice to hear you are close to your parents. I think communication between a parent and child is of extreme importance." Mom's glare let me know I was in deeper trouble. Mom was okay with the omission when things were casual, but Levi was acting like we were moving in together or something.

"Well, I'd like to meet your parents, Levi. Just name the time and place," Dad said.

"I will. My parents will be thrilled."

"Excuse me." Throwing my napkin down on the table, I pushed back my chair and headed for the bathroom. I couldn't believe Levi was playing this game. Why did he care that I didn't mention him? It was just a summer fling, right?

After taking a moment to get my anger in check I returned to the table with a huge smile plastered on my face. "Honey, we're going to be late, aren't we?"

"For what?" Levi asked, watching me closely as I sat down.

"That thing we just couldn't miss." I shot Levi a look to kill and he got the hint.

"Oh yeah."

"Well, we don't want to keep you kids, let's get the check," Dad said.

Ten minutes later we headed for the door and noticed the torrential rainstorm.

"I didn't know it was going to rain," Mom said as we got ready to venture out.

"It's just how things are here. It can go from a clear sky to a storm in minutes," I explained as if I was the resident New Orleans expert.

"We might as well get it over with," Dad said.

"Okay, thanks for dinner. I won't be back too late, Mom."

"All right, have a nice night you two." Mom waved before dashing out.

As soon as my parents disappeared around the corner, I walked out into the rain pulling Levi with me.

"What the hell was all of that? What are you playing at?"

"What am I playing at? I can't believe you didn't tell your parents about me!"

"What the heck was I supposed to tell them? It's not like we're officially together or anything."

"Not officially together? You mean I've been staying away from other girls all summer just for the fun of it?"

The rain pouring down only accentuated the anger on Levi's face.

"It's not like I've been with anyone else either."

"Then what are we arguing about? That we're both too stubborn to admit we actually have something here?"

"What does it matter? I mean it's already August—"

"Just stop. I know what the problem is."

"Care to enlighten me?" Already soaked to the bone, I could hardly contain my anger.

Levi came out of left field. "Let me take you out on a real date."

"Seriously? That's your response? And what separates a real date from anything else?"

"Dinner, wine, nice clothes. Come on, it'll be fun."

I paused, fleetingly wondering if I really wanted to say no even if I had the willpower to resist him. I admitted defeat, "Fine."

"So Friday night at seven?"

"Okay. Are we done here 'cause this rain is getting old and—"

With the rain enveloping us, Levi interrupted me with a kiss. Holding back for a moment, I couldn't resist any longer. I wrapped my arms around his neck, pulling him down to my level. A honking car brought us back to reality and he pulled away from me slowly, his gaze heated.

"I guess I should get you out of the rain."

"You mean us?"

"No, just you. The rain doesn't bother me much."

"Why doesn't that surprise me?"

"With me babe, the surprises never end." With an arm draped over my shoulders, he led me back to the hotel.

***

"That was fast," Mom said as I walked into the room.

"Yeah, we decided not to go."

"Probably for the best, considering you're drenched." She tried to hide a small smile.

"Good point. I'm going to go dry off."

"Do that. But Allie?"

"Yeah?" I asked as I headed to my room.

"I think I like him for you."

"What does that mean?"

"You could do worse. Much worse."

"It doesn't matter. I'm leaving soon anyway."

"Not everything in life is black and white. Sometimes the best parts are gray. Just remember that not everything can fit into one your neat little boxes."

"My neat little boxes?"

She laughed lightly. "Just think about it."

"Okay. If you are done philosophizing, I'm going to change."

Mom left the next morning and I couldn't get her words out of my head. I wasn't completely sure what she was getting at, but I was determined not to let the fact that I was leaving get in the way of the time we did have. In just the last few months both my mom and best friend had accused me of being unable to color outside the lines, and by God I was going to prove them wrong.

Fourteen

The dress demanded to be worn. Determined to wear something completely different from the bright colored sundresses that filled most of my closet, the short, black, and lacy dress I bought with Hailey called out to me. Slipping into the little black dress, I wondered what Levi had planned for the night.

I used more dramatic makeup than usual and put on a new pair of kitten heel pumps. Leaving my hair down, I was ready just as Levi knocked.

"Hello there gorgeous," Levi gaped at me unabashedly.

"You don't look so bad yourself." Levi looked great in a dress shirt and khakis.

"You ready?"

"Definitely."

He took my hand as we boarded the elevator, smiling at me in a way that gave me chills.

"Are you cold?"

"No."

"Does that mean I'm the cause of the goose bumps?"

"Maybe," I said coyly.

"Nice." He gave me one of his devastating toothy grins.

An older couple entered the elevator one floor down, disrupting our conversation.

"Celebrating something special tonight?" the woman asked.

"No, just a night out," I answered.

"There is always something worth celebrating," she continued.

"Right," I said as the elevator door opened up at the lobby. "Have a nice night."

"You too," she smiled.

We walked out into the sticky heat of the night, headed for dinner.

Levi squeezed my hand. "You were wrong, you know."

"About what?"

"We are celebrating tonight."

"Oh yeah? What are we celebrating exactly?"

"We're celebrating you," he stopped walking to place a hand over my heart, "and me, and an amazing summer."

"All things worth celebrating."

We walked the rest of the way to the restaurant in near silence, just enjoying each other's company. Usually Levi felt the need to fill every second with conversation, and it was a nice change to just exist.

The ambiance at Antoine's was perfect. Seated at a corner table, I was struck by the beauty of the historic restaurant. With a menu of French-Creole food, Levi had picked the perfect place.

The waiter approached our table shortly after we sat down. "Welcome to Antoine's. Can I get you something to drink?"

"Yes, we'll have the 1982 Chateau Mouton Rothschild." Levi ordered without glancing at the wine menu.

"Nice choice, I will be back with it shortly." By the expression on the waiter's face I knew it must be really expensive.

"So you know a lot about wine?" I asked.

"You could say that." He smiled.

"What do you mean?"

"My family is originally from France, and we still have some vineyards in Bordeaux."

"Oh, wow. That's really cool."

"Yeah, it's a very beautiful area; we'll have to visit sometime."

The waiter returned with the wine and I watched as Levi got serious when he tasted it. "Yes, perfect, thank you."

This really was a different side of Levi, and I liked it.

After the waiter retreated, Levi held up his glass reminding me of the night we toasted with coffee.

"To a truly amazing summer and to many more celebrations," Levi said lightly before we clinked glasses.

He watched me intently as I took a sip. "What do you think?"

"Wow, that's really smooth." Even with my limited experience with wine, I knew this was a good one.

"I thought it was perfect for tonight."

I smiled, picking up a menu.

"You don't need that." Levi took the menu from my hands placing it on the table next to me. The waiter appeared immediately.

"Are you ready to order?"

"Yes. We'll start with the huîtres a la Rockefeller and escargot la bordelaise. Then we'll both have the Chateaubriand."

Prepared to argue with his presumption that he could order for me, I stopped myself realizing that if he was even half as good at ordering dinner as he was at picking wine, I was in good hands.

Finishing my first glass of wine right as the appetizers arrived, Levi refilled my glass.

"Okay, the Oysters Rockefeller are incredible," I said between bites.

"The dish was invented here."

"Really? That's cool."

The rest of the meal was equally as good. We shared an entrée designed for two, and there was something intimate about sharing with him that just added to the setting.

"I have something for you." Levi glanced at me nervously, an expression that looked wrong on his face. I didn't like it.

"Really? You didn't have to get me anything."

"It's actually a family piece but it was made for you."

"Levi… I can't take anything like that."

"Shh. Just let me enjoy giving it to you, okay?"

"Okay." I smiled.

He pulled out a small box from his pocket and my breath hitched, Levi didn't seem like the jewelry type.

He gently opened the box, pulling out a small ring covered in tiny rubies. Before I could even react, he slid the gorgeous ring on my left hand. "Perfect." He smiled contently, all evidence of nerves gone.

"Levi, it's beautiful, but I can't take it." I moved to remove it from my finger, but he stopped me.

"It looks perfect, doesn't it? Do you like it?"

"I love it. Red is my favorite color, you know."

"I know."

I wasn't completely comfortable wearing a ring on my left ring finger but I didn't want to insult him by moving it. It wasn't like he had proposed or anything, it was just a gift and making a big deal out of it would just ruin the night.

"Thank you. It's beautiful and I'll treasure it."

"I'm glad."

Overwhelmed by the gift I let the words on my mind slip out. "I can't believe the summer is almost over, it went so fast."

"Entirely too fast."

"So what happens now? Or when I leave?" I bit my tongue, hoping I hadn't just spoiled the evening.

"We'll make it work."

"You think?"

"I know."

"I guess at least we don't have to worry about airfare if you want to come to visit." I laughed lightly.

"Let's not even think about it now. Just enjoy tonight." He took my hand again, running a finger over the small stones of the ring.

"You're absolutely right." As I said the words aloud, they echoed in my head. No matter what happened between Levi and me after I left, I was going to enjoy the time we had together. The heated look Levi gave me let me know he was thinking the same thing.

"Do you want dessert?" he asked as the last of our dinner dishes were cleared away.

I paused momentarily. "Maybe later."

"Good, I agree completely."

Signaling for the waiter, Levi never took his eyes off me. He paid the check and we headed out.

The electricity between us sizzled as we walked hand in hand through Jackson Square. Without warning, Levi yanked my hand pulling me into Pirates alley, right off the square. Pushing me against the bars of the railing, he pinned one of my arms above my head. I held onto a bar with the

182

other, steading myself as he moved his face close to mine. With his other hand, he pulled my body towards him.

Shivering with anticipation, I didn't let my eyes leave his gaze. When the kiss came it was as aggressive as the way he held me—unyielding. Without waiting, he pushed into my mouth, deepening the kiss quickly. Groaning, he pulled me even closer, his hands holding me possessively. I gave myself over to him completely, wanting him more than I thought possible. His hands roamed and as he broke the kiss, I opened my eyes slowly.

His eyes held an unasked question and finding the answer he was looking for, he quickly unbuttoned his dress shirt, pulling it off to reveal a white tank. He started kissing me again, and I instinctively closed my eyes, barely registering us leaving the ground until we were on my balcony a near split second later.

Levi pushed open the door and we stumbled backwards into the room. Closing the door with his foot, Levi moved us toward my bedroom. I slipped off my shoes, dropping my bag.

Never taking his eyes off me, he unzipped my dress, letting it fall to the floor. He kissed my neck as his fingers found the clasp of my bra. I pulled the shirt over his head, relieved to finally have his bare skin against mine. He tilted my head up towards him, kissing me again as my arms wound around his neck.

All at once he intensified the kiss while picking me up. I wrapped my legs around him as he carried me over to the bed, placing me down gently before leaning over me with a faint smile that left nothing to the imagination.

Fifteen

There was something so natural about waking up in Levi's arms. I snuggled into him as he kissed the top of my head. Rolling over I looked at him, enjoying the look of contentment on his face. I had a sudden feeling that this was the *real* Levi. Maybe it was his rumpled hair, or the sleepiness still evident in his eyes, but there was a rawness about him that made it hard to believe he was the same arrogant man I met at the beginning of the summer.

"Good morning, beautiful," he said playfully, picking up a few strands of my hair where they lay on the pillow.

"Good morning." I smiled.

There wasn't even an ounce of awkwardness between us. You would have thought we had been waking up next to one another for years. I laughed to myself remembering that this was actually the second time we'd awoken together.

"You are so beautiful when you sleep," he said quietly.

"You watched me sleep?"

"Yeah, I couldn't resist. It's not often I'm around you when you aren't being all feisty and defensive. It was nice to see you completely peaceful for a change."

"I didn't get to see you sleep... too bad."

"You can always watch tonight."

"Tonight? What makes you think this is ever going to happen again?"

He raised an eyebrow "Sweetheart, you and I both know that there was nothing one time about last night."

I knew he was right and said nothing, realizing my silence was tantamount to agreement.

"How about we just stay here all day?" he asked, pulling me up on top of him.

I rolled off him. "Very funny. You know I have to meet Hailey for brunch." I looked at the clock on the bed stand. "Wow, I need to meet her soon, we slept late."

"Yeah, I guess we did. You could always call and cancel."

"Cancel on Hailey?" I said skeptically

"Okay, maybe not. She'll blame me and I'll be the one dealing with it." He laughed.

"Besides, you have plans this morning too, don't you?"

"As if I would choose basketball with the guys over this?"

"Well, either way I'm going, so you need to leave."

"Fine. But we're having dinner tonight. I have something to talk to you about."

"Dinner sounds good, but what do you need to tell me?" I asked curiously.

"Relax, it's a good thing." Levi fingered the ruby ring. "This looks good on you."

186

"Thanks, I like it." I had nearly forgotten the ring with such a whirlwind evening, but it looked just as beautiful in the morning.

"I'm glad." Levi watched as I slipped out of bed to find some clothes to throw on.

"If you're done staring, get dressed." I tossed his pants at him.

Catching them in one hand, he grudgingly got out of the bed and started dressing. "Okay, okay. Are you always this bossy in the morning?"

"I'm not exactly used to having company this early."

"Too bad, you're going to have to get used to it." He winked, fishing his shirt off the floor.

Pulling me into his arms, he trailed light kisses from my ear to my neck, almost making me forget how late I was running.

I pushed him away. "You better stop that, or we're never getting out of here."

"My thoughts exactly."

"Levi, come on."

"All right, I'm going. How about I meet you around six?"

"Okay, I'll see you then."

I walked Levi through the living area and to the door. With his hand on the doorknob he paused. "For the record, that was the best night ever. I'm going to spend the day thinking of ways to make tonight even better."

"Good-bye, Levi."

"Bye love, don't miss me too much."

Shaking my head, I closed the door and headed to the shower, letting my giddiness surface now that Levi wasn't there to watch.

***

Parking on the street about half a block from the Columns Hotel, I walked briskly up the front steps. I scanned the dining room, my gaze settling on a small table where Hailey sat studying a menu.

"I'm so sorry I'm late!" I apologized taking a seat across from her.

"It's okay. Have a good night?" she asked inquisitively.

"A very good night."

"That sounds promising. Care to share?" She pursed her lips like she honestly expected me to hold back on her.

"It was incredible. Every moment of the night was spot on. It was the most amazing date ever. And Levi wasn't even Levi if that makes sense."

Hailey laughed. "Where did he take you?"

"Antoine's. The food and wine were fantastic."

"He was showing off. Feel very special, he never takes girls there." She smiled.

"How would you even know?"

"I'm around him enough to notice those things. Anyway, did you guys do anything after? If he was trying that hard, there has to be more."

188

"No, not really," I said, trying to change the conversation before we entered way too much information territory. I knew that Levi wasn't Hailey's brother, but I was pretty sure it would have the same weirdness for her.

"Well, I'm glad things are working out with you two."

"Me too, although it's going to make leaving even harder."

"You could always just stay here."

"No I can't. I have to start school in a few weeks."

"I know; it was just wishful thinking. I ordered us champagne by the way," she explained right before a waitress set down two flutes on the table.

"Thank you." I smiled at the waitress as she walked away. I was smiling at everyone.

"Okay, let's toast."

"What should we toast?" I asked.

"To amazing dates and incredible friendships."

"All right." I held up my champagne ready to clink glasses with Hailey but her glass never connected with mine.

Hailey stilled. "Did Levi give you that ring?"

"Yeah. He said it's a family ring or something but he really wanted me to have it."

"Oh." She bit her lip nervously.

"What's wrong? What aren't you telling me?" I placed my glass on the table, starting to worry.

"Levi didn't explain its significance?"

My stomach sank. "What significance?"

"He wasn't making up the family ring part. Except it's more than that. It's *the* ring. The future leader gives it to his intended."

"What!" I said louder than I meant to and people from the surrounding tables turned to stare. I lowered my voice. "What are you talking about? Future leader?"

"Calm down. He must really like you, but you can always give it back."

I struggled to remove the ring from my finger but it wouldn't budge. "What the hell? Hailey it won't come off!"

She paled. "When you said you had an amazing night, you didn't mean *that* amazing of a night, right?" She looked at me questioningly and I was afraid of what she would ask next. "I mean you didn't sleep with him, did you?"

"What does that matter?"

"Oh my god, you consummated it. Oh my god. Levi did that without telling you... unbelievable."

"Consummated it? What the hell are you talking about?"

"You can't give the ring back, Allie. Spending the night with him kind of made it permanent."

"Permanent?" Heat flooded me and the room started to spin. I was terrified to hear her response.

"As in you are now his mate and he can't take another. There'll have to be an official

190

celebration… Wow I don't even know what to say."

"You have got to be joking! I didn't agree to this and why would Levi want to make me his… Uggh I can't even say the word. Get this damn ring off me!"

"It's not going to come off, it's permanent. You have to stay here with him now. Oh my god, I knew he was crazy about you, but I can't believe he did this. Levi has done stupid things, but this is way beyond anything—"

"Please tell me this is a joke. Please." I started feeling hot.

"I'm sorry."

"I can't do this. I can't do this." I stood up quickly, knocking over my glass of champagne. I had to get out of there.

"Allie, wait!" Hailey called after me but I ran down the corridor.

Dashing down the street, I jumped in the car, starting it without looking behind me. I had no idea where I was going, but I had to get away from the craziness. There was no way I was buying anything they were selling.

Sitting at a stoplight I struggled with the ring again, using my nails to try to pry it off, but it did nothing. Tears nearly blinded me as I drove through the city haphazardly. There had to be a way to get the ring off, because there was no way I was spending time with anyone who would trick me like that. It just didn't make sense. Levi could have any girl, why would he need to trap me?

Still unsure of where to go, I knew I had to leave New Orleans. I couldn't risk going back to the hotel and running into any Pterons. For all I knew, Natalie was in on it. I'd just have to buy the necessities I needed on the road.

Memories of the summer flooded me as I tried to understand how I could have fallen under Levi's spell. Maybe it was all part of him being supernatural. I hoped I was right because I didn't want to believe it was my own mistake that got me into the mess.

Sixteen

The monotony of the interstate helped calm my nerves enough for me to make a plan. I was going home and getting as far away from Levi as possible. There had to be some way to remove the ring. I wanted to believe that Hailey had made it all up, but I knew she hadn't. It all fit. Levi's nerves before he gave me the ring, his comment about needing to talk to me that night—he was probably going to drop the bomb about what he'd done. What I couldn't understand was why he would want to trap me. Sure, there was chemistry between us, but we had only known each other a few months. It didn't make any sense.

I called Mom, dialing my house number with absolutely no idea what I was going to tell her. After three rings I expected the machine to pick up, but instead an unfamiliar male voice said "Hello?"

"Hi." I wondered if I had hit the wrong contact on my phone. "Is Diane there?"

"Allie?"

"Yeah."

"Hey, it's Andrew."

"Andrew Thomas? What are you doing at my house?" I asked, completely taken aback that one of my least favorite acquaintances from high school was answering my home phone.

"Didn't your mom tell you about her and my dad?"

"She said they were dating, but why are you there?" I repeated, getting frustrated.

"We're staying here while we redo the kitchen at our house."

"Oh… I didn't know."

"Yeah, my dad says he'd never be able to sell it without some upgrades."

"Sell it?" I asked fearful of the response I would get.

"Your mom really didn't mention it? My dad's probably moving in with your mom once we leave for school in the fall."

"No. I guess she forgot to mention that," I said angrily. And my mom got mad at me for not telling her about Levi? What else was she keeping from me?

"Geez, that must be weird. But on a good note, we'll get to hang out on breaks and I think our parents are planning a cool vacation for winter break for all of us."

"Seriously?"

"Yup. Cool, right?"

Nothing about it sounded cool.

He continued. "By the way, you have an awesome DVD collection in your room."

"You've been in my room?"

"Yeah… it's not a big deal, right?"

"I've got to go." I hung up without waiting for his response. I felt sick. The thought of going home no longer appealed. Andrew was a total jerk most of the time, and never stopped bothering me. I considered where else I could go.

My mind clouded with dark thoughts, and I needed a distraction. I needed ice cream. Not just any ice cream, I needed a hot fudge sundae. There was nothing like it to help drown your sorrows. Of course, the craving hit me just after passing Chattanooga and miles from Knoxville.

As I drove through the middle of nowhere, scanning every sign advertising food, I was almost able to forget about the stupid ring. I flipped through the channels on the radio, frustrated by every song that came on. Who would have thought it was possible for so many songs to be about taking it slow? After giving up on the radio, I saw a sign for Dairy Queen. Even though it was half a mile from the exit, I couldn't pass it up.

Pulling into a spot in the nearly empty lot, I took a deep breath and tried to focus on the task at hand. Find a bathroom, get some ice cream, and get as far from New Orleans and Levi as possible.

The Dairy Queen was the kind connected to a small gas station and convenience store. On a Sunday I would have expected a post lunch crowd, but I was the only customer. The clerk disappeared as soon as she handed me my cup of vanilla ice cream with gobs of hot fudge (I had asked for extra) so I took a seat at a small table by the window.

Indulging in the first creamy bite, I tried to pretend that the events of the past few hours hadn't happened. The problem was that I wore a constant reminder of it on my left hand. I sat on my hand to avoid the temptation to keep trying to pull it off. My finger was getting sore from messing with it so much.

After only a few bites of ice cream the bell above the door jingled, signaling the arrival of more customers. I heard mumbled voices and assumed the new arrivals were ordering.

"Hello there sugar," a deep voice drawled from right behind me.

I fought the urge to turn around and instead took another bite.

"Oh, come on now, I know you heard me."

I bristled as I heard a chair scrape the floor. Great. He was going to try to sit with me.

"So what's your name?"

Clearly, ignoring him wasn't going to work.

"Listen, I'm not in the mood—" I faltered when I saw the hulk of a man seated across from me. Unshaven, with shaggy hair and a worn out t-shirt, the guy wasn't a pretty sight. I hoped my usual evasion tactics worked this time. A quick survey made it clear he wasn't alone. Two other men stood behind me now. Fear crept up on me as I realized that I was being sized up.

"You were saying?" His wry smile did nothing to relax me.

"Hey, nice ring baby." My eyes darted toward the voice, and I noticed a pair of incredibly dirty jeans. One of the friends now hovered beside me, boxing me in.

"You can have it if I can ever get the damn thing off."

I stood up and prepared to throw my ice cream in the trash. "Excuse me."

"You are definitely not excused." The first man smiled and ran his hands through his greasy hair.

"Hey Harriston, that's what I think it is right?" My exit was blocked by the second man.

"No question, I wonder what this little princess is doing out here alone. Trevor is going to be happy with us, very happy with us."

"I need to go." The hairs stood up on the back of my neck, things weren't looking good. Suddenly being back in New Orleans didn't sound so bad.

"You're not going anywhere other than with us. You sure you don't want to finish that ice cream?" The original man, who was evidently named Harriston, smirked.

I tried to hide my fear. "I've lost my appetite."

"Well then, I guess we'll be going." Harriston grabbed me roughly by the arm. "You are going to come with us nicely, little girl."

"I'm not going anywhere with you." I looked around, figuring that someone had to see what was going on, but the cashier was missing. Two other large men stood at the door, and by their mocking expressions, I deduced they were part of the same group.

"Hey, leave me the hell—"

A dirty hand covered my mouth. "No one's coming to your rescue. Better make it easier on yourself." Harriston pushed something cold and metal against the back of my neck. "I have no problem cutting you; you're still worth a lot roughed up."

I nodded as Harriston led me out to the parking lot. I gazed longingly at my Land Rover as we stopped in front of a rusted out old Chevy pickup.

"Get some tape," Harriston ordered and removed his hand from my mouth to quickly replace it with a strip of duct tape. He let go of my arms long enough to tie my hands and feet together. I tried to fight them by flailing but they just tied the rope tighter, making it dig into the skin of my wrists. The next time I flailed, all I accomplished was losing my flip-flops and gaining a small cut from the knife.

"I hope you don't mind riding in the back, sugar." His sinister tobacco stained smile suggested he didn't care what I thought.

"I'll ride in back with her," the guy with the filthy jeans said.

"She's your type, huh, Riley?"

"Exactly my type." Riley picked me up and jumped into the back, looking down at me the whole time. He was younger and appeared less threatening than Harriston, but I knew he could be just as dangerous. He put me down before sitting next to me.

A door slammed shut. The engine started up after a few tries and the truck noisily sped out of the parking lot.

Riley didn't say anything for a while, he just looked at me, but as the truck continued to travel, he decided to open his mouth.

"You're really pretty. I wish I knew your name."

Obviously, I couldn't answer him with my mouth taped so he continued.

"I wish you were my girl. I'd take better care of you than your boyfriend. Why would he let you wander by yourself? I would never let you out of my sight."

I wondered why he assumed I had a boyfriend, was all this somehow related to Levi? As angry as I was at him, I could have used him at that moment.

The truck started to bump up and down, and I was thrown against the side painfully. I had the impression we were on a dirt road.

I shivered involuntarily as I thought about where they might be taking me.

Riley scooted over to pick me up. "It's okay baby, I've got you." He moved my hair to examine the small cut left by the knife. I hoped I was bleeding all over him; it served him right. As if to prove his point about "having me" Riley started to let his hands rove up my legs. I really regretted wearing a short sundress. I tried to scream in protest but the tape limited me to mumbles.

"I can see why he picked you. I'd have picked you too if I were him. Maybe you won't go back to

199

him. Maybe Trevor will let me keep you." Riley smiled happily and I started having visions of being kept on a leash like a pet. Damn, how did I get in this situation? Me and my craving for ice cream.

Just as I thought I couldn't take any more time spent with Riley's dirty hands all over my legs, the truck came to a stop. In one motion, Riley scooped me up, stood, and jumped out.

"Looks like Trevor's already home," Harriston called as he headed toward a rustic cabin. That's when it clicked; I was essentially living in my own horror movie. Trevor was going to be some lunatic that wore human skin as a mask or mutilated girls for sport. I was petrified. Looking around me I noticed giant cats, or really more like mountain lions moving in toward us.

Harriston entered the cabin leaving the door open behind him for Riley to enter.

From my position in Riley's arms, I looked around me. The large room was surprisingly well furnished. It didn't fit. Several couches and armchairs filled the room with a large area rug on the floor. The furnishings did nothing to cover up the squeaky floorboards. It seemed like whoever owned the place was trying to show off. Several men walked into the room, all of whom were shirtless. Fantastic.

"We brought you something, Trevor," Harriston said blocking me from the man's view.

"I told you I didn't want anything from Dairy Queen."

"I think you'll like this one." Harriston moved aside and Riley stepped forward. "Put her down, idiot."

Riley set me on my feet but with them tied together I swayed for a moment. He grabbed me before I could fall.

The man I could only assume was Trevor approached me. "I admit she's a looker, but I can get my own women."

"One with that kind of ring?" Harriston challenged.

Trevor pulled my bound hands toward him. "Since when did Levi get a mate and what the hell is she doing this far from New Orleans?" My chest tightened. They definitely knew what the ring was.

"Only thing to do is ask," Trevor said. "I'm going to take this tape off baby, I'll make it fast."

"Ow!" I yelled as the tape ripped from my face.

"That tape was such a waste of those lips. I may have to rectify that later." Trevor watched me with a heated gaze. I was pretty sure he was undressing me in his head. With rugged features, tar black hair, and intense blue eyes that looked at me like I was prey, Trevor screamed intimidation. He stroked my face with his hand.

I shook my head trying to knock his hand away. "Get your hands off me!"

"No, I don't think I want to do that, but how about I untie your feet?" Without waiting for an answer, he bent down and began untying the knot at my feet, spending way too much time on it. His hands grazed my legs as he stood up. Ugh. "I'll untie your hands too if you promise to be good. I'm guessing that rope doesn't feel too good on your wrists."

"What do you care?" I was now completely surrounded by large men, I tried to calm my breathing.

"I'm only trying to be a good host."

"Host? You mean kidnapper."

"It's all in the terminology," Trevor said as he untied my wrists. "So why did he pick you? Other than the obvious, of course." He gestured up and down my body.

"Why did who pick me?"

"Don't play stupid."

"Then spell it out for me."

"You're wearing the ring of the Pteron ruling family. Why did the prince pick you?"

Prince? Hailey had said he was the future leader, but a prince? "Listen. This is all a big misunderstanding. Levi never even told me what the ring meant. Had I known, I wouldn't have accepted it. I'm just a girl from New York who wants to get home." I realized after the words left my mouth, that I was probably giving too much information.

"Wait, are you trying to tell me you were duped into accepting the ring? You had no idea when you jumped into bed with the prince that you'd leave it his princess?" Trevor's laughter was deep and primal.

"That's exactly what I'm saying. So would you please just let me go?"

"Why would that change anything?"

"What do you want from me? What can you possibly gain by holding me here?"

"You really don't realize how much you're worth, do you?"

Something told me I didn't want to know.

Seventeen

"You didn't find a tracker on her?" Trevor asked while I still processed his comment about my worth.

"No. But we never thought to check her," Riley admitted.

"Are you idiots? You think he didn't leave something on her?" A small smile spread on his lips. "I guess I'll have to do it myself."

"Hell no. Whatever you are thinking, keep your hands to yourself. Besides, he didn't put a tracker on me. He only gave me the ring last night."

"Wow, and you ran out on him that quickly? Oh wait, you did it when you found out the truth, huh?"

"I don't want to talk about it." I was hanging on by a thread; discussing Levi anymore threatened to push me over the edge.

"We can do this the easy way or the hard way," he sneered.

"Do what?"

"Take off your dress," he ordered.

"Excuse me? Do you really think I'm that stupid? No way!"

"Like I said, we can do this the easy way or hard way. Either you take it off or I do, and I really don't mind."

There were at least ten men in the room by this point. "You honestly expect me to take off my

204

clothes in a room full of men?" I wondered where all these guys were coming from.

"Yes, of course, I do," he said without hesitation.

"First, tell me, who are you?" I needed to stall him.

"I'm Trevor, I thought that was clear."

"Not your name. Okay, I guess I mean *what* are you?" They knew about Levi so I assumed they were more than they seemed.

Trevor smiled. "Don't you know?"

"If I knew why would I be asking?"

"Didn't you notice anything outside?"

"No way… Are you guys tigers or something?"

"Did you see stripes? No, we're not tigers, we're cougars, or mountain lions, or panthers, or pumas. Whatever colloquial term you like."

"Oh."

"'Oh' is right."

"So you really can change into a cougar?"

Trevor smiled. "If I didn't know you were sleeping with a Pteron, I'd think you had never seen a shifter before."

"I'm still new to all of this, and besides Pterons don't actually shift into birds." I decided not to mention that I'd seen wolves shift.

"No more stalling."

"Stalling?"

Trevor smiled again. "Yes. You think I don't know what you're doing?"

Damn. "Listen, I don't have a tracking device on me. I've already been tricked and kidnapped enough for one day. Can't you let me keep my dignity?" Real and intense fear engulfed me.

"Either take off your dress or I'll do it for you."

"No." There was no way I was taking off my clothes.

"Don't say I didn't warn you." He reached for my dress, ripping the fabric easily. With one more swift motion, I was left standing in only a bra and panties. All eyes were on me and I wanted to sink into the floor. I shuddered, noticing the hungry looks of the men surrounding me as I attempted to cover myself with my hands.

"Hot pink, huh? Maybe I'll have to organize some alone time for us before we turn you over." Leering, Trevor reached out a hand to touch me. I slapped it away.

"Oh, you want to play that way?" He reached out and grabbed my wrists. Another man handed him the rope so he could rebind my hands. "I told you to be good."

"Please, just let me go," I whimpered. I was ready to do anything to avoid any further undressing.

Trevor studied me for a moment. "Okay, I'll compromise."

"Compromise?"

"Riley, take her into one of the back rooms and finish the search." Trevor smiled.

"What! You call that a compromise!?"

"Would you prefer to have it done in front of everyone? Better yet, is it that you're disappointed it won't be me?" Trevor taunted.

"It's okay, baby. I won't hurt you," Riley said as he took my arm. As much as I wanted to fight, I figured one guy's grubby hands were better than a room full of guys watching, or worse, participating.

Catcalls followed as Riley led me out of the room. So far I was wearing as much as I would have on at the beach, but I knew it was about to get worse.

Riley led me into a bedroom with several bunk beds lining the walls. I shivered from fear and not the cold.

"Shh, it's okay." Riley tried to comfort me. He looked torn.

I couldn't help it and started to cry. I just couldn't take anymore, especially not that kind of violation.

"I'm sorry about this." With my hands still bound, I could do nothing to cover myself as he prepared to unclasp my bra. The sense of violation burned and the tears fell hot and fast. Fear of what might come next kept me as still as a statue.

"You don't have anything on you, do you?" Riley asked as he brushed tears off my face. His actions were much gentler than I expected. "I don't want to make this any worse for you."

"I don't have a tracker. I swear."

"Okay, I'll take your word for it."

"What?" Relief flooded me but I was looking for a catch.

"But there are a few conditions."

"Conditions?" I bristled; afraid his conditions would be worse than a more thorough pat down.

"Yes. Some conditions," he repeated.

"What are they?"

"You let everyone think I finished the search. I'd be up a creek if Trevor found out, and you would just have to deal him doing it himself."

"Okay, I'll agree to that, but what else?" I asked nervously. I didn't want to know the other conditions.

"Tell me your name."

"You want to know my name?"

"Yeah. I want to put a name to your face."

Stunned with disbelief I answered. "Allie. My name is Allie."

"Allie? I like that. Allie. A pretty name for a pretty girl. It's nice to meet you, Allie." He held out his hand to shake mine and then dropped it down after realizing my hands were still tied. "Sorry."

I nodded, terrified of making him back out of the deal. "Is that it?"

"Oh, I might call in a favor later." He ran a finger down the side of my face, and I tensed wondering what the favor would be. "Come on, we need to get back. Remember what I told you." Riley took my arm pulling me back out to the open area.

Another round of catcalls awaited us. "Are you sure we have to give her to the Blackwells?" someone yelled.

"Yes, and in the same condition we got her." I couldn't ignore the heated look Trevor gave me.

"Did she feel as good as she looks?" Harriston said with a harsh smile.

"Of course she did," Riley said with a much more confident voice than he used with me. "And she enjoyed it. Said she'd stay with me if she could."

"Did she now?" Trevor asked, coming closer to us. I flinched as he brought his arm towards me but relaxed as he wrapped a blanket around my shoulders. I let out a sigh of relief; maybe the worst was over.

"Yes, she did." Riley avoided my eye. I understood he wanted to be convincing but this was ridiculous.

"Is that right?"

I tried to muster a confident voice. "You know, I've always been a cat person…" I shrugged awkwardly, careful not to lose the blanket.

The room erupted into laughter.

"Nice to know you have a sense of humor."

"Yeah, I have a really great personality usually, that is when I'm not being held captive." I couldn't believe I was acting so calm, but breaking down would only make escape less likely.

"Trevor, I've got the Blackwells on the line," one guy called, holding up a cell phone. I was surprised they even had service out there.

"You might as well sit down, this might take a while." Trevor pushed me down onto a couch. Readjusting the blanket around me, Riley sat down next to me almost protectively before anyone else could.

I shot him a dirty look for his earlier performance and he winked. I decided to let it go and let the guy feed his ego. Maybe he'd forget about the favor.

Struggling to hear Trevor's conversation from across the room, I wanted to yell at the rest of the men to shut up, but I didn't want to draw any more attention to myself. Thankfully, Trevor took care of the noise himself. "Enough!" he bellowed.

"Sorry about that. As I was saying, I have someone of extreme value in my possession right now." He paused, likely listening to the caller on the other end of the line. "Before I give any details, let me emphasize that as far as anyone is concerned our hands are clean, she came willingly."

What the hell? I wanted to scream but before I could argue, Riley had his hand over my mouth. Arrg, for the second time today I had a dirty hand on my mouth.

"What would the mate of Levi Laurent be worth to you?"

210

"Trust me. It's his mate. The reason you haven't heard is that it just happened last night." Trevor glanced at me. "There is no question it's the ring."

"Not so fast. What will you give me?"

"Bull. She's worth a hell of a lot more than that to you. I want 1.5."

"Don't insult me, 750 Gs for a chance to run the show? I'll take a cool mil, that's my final offer or I call the Dalys."

"Fine. But I want the money first."

Trevor hung up the phone and strolled over to me. Riley removed his hand. "Thanks sweetheart, you just made me a lot of money."

"Don't call me sweetheart!" I'd had enough of the fake endearments.

"Wow, down girl," he said as he mimed cracking a whip. A few men laughed.

"So they really agreed to a million, Trevor?" Harriston asked, licking his lips.

"I could have pushed him harder but I didn't want him to call my bluff. I don't want to mess with the Dalys."

"You can't be serious? Why would anyone pay that kind of money for me?" The only person in the world *that* interested in me was my father, and I knew he wasn't on the other end of the phone.

"You are the prince's mate. He can't take another. Without you, there is no heir and the Laurent line dies out. The other high ranking Pterons would pay a lot to get control of you."

"You mean kill me."

"No, you are worth more alive. Theoretically if you died by hands other than his own, your boyfriend could take another mate if he got hold of the ring."

"Okay, slow down. Why do you keep calling him a prince?" I was still trying to figure out how all these people tied together.

"You have to be kidding me." He wrinkled his brow in confusion.

"Just pretend for a second that I'm not."

"You had no idea you were involved with the crown prince of the Pterons?"

"Um, no. I thought we already established that. So you think of him as royalty too?"

"Yes. Unfortunately, the Pterons have been in control for years. Really, it's all been in the hands of the Laurents."

I didn't know what to say. Once again, I was discovering something that Levi should have told me himself.

Trevor noticed my expression. "Relax princess, there's no reason to worry about Levi, you're never going to see him again anyway."

"If I am so important, don't you think he's going to come after me?" I asked, not so sure of it myself.

"Only if he can find you."

"And you don't think he will?"

"Not before the Blackwells get here. The family was quite anxious to get you in their hands; they have already sent some expendables to get you."

"Expendables?"

"You don't think the family wants their own hands dirty in a kidnapping? No. These families have others to do their dirty work." A look crossed Trevor's face and I sensed there was more to his words than he was telling me.

I looked out into the darkening sky hoping like hell I would find a way out of the mess I was in.

"So what now?"

"We wait. Can I get you something to drink?"

"Seriously? How about untying my hands again?"

"No, I don't think so."

"Please? Just for a few minutes?"

"What could you possibly expect to do with your hands for a few minutes… oh wait, can't keep your hands off Riley huh?"

"Gross. He wishes." I ignored Riley's grunt beside me. "I need to use the bathroom, okay?"

"Well, you'll just have to do it with your hands tied. Riley, why don't you help her?"

"No, on second thought I'll hold it."

"You think it's going to be better where you're going next?"

I'll take my chances. Of course, I didn't plan on going with the Blackwells; I just had no idea how I

213

was going to avoid it. I just wished I wouldn't have to make a break for it with a full bladder.

"Come on Trevor, can't the girl use the bathroom? With all of us in here what's she going to do?" Riley argued.

"I suppose we should be good hosts. Be my guest."

I let out a sigh of relief as Riley steered me out of the room again. He led me up a staircase and gestured to a small bathroom. Ugh. The place was disgusting but beggars can't be choosers.

"My hands?" I asked, holding them out to him.

"Don't cause any trouble."

"I wouldn't dream of it."

Eighteen

Looking out the small window of the bathroom into the darkness, I noticed a bird fly past. I couldn't be sure, but it was the right size for a crow. I hoped like I never had before that I was right. As angry as I was with Levi, I'd rather take my chances with his family and friends than these Blackwells, whoever they were. Quietly I pushed against the glass but it wouldn't give. It didn't matter anyway, since it was far too small for me to fit through.

I looked at the dirty toilet, debating how badly I needed to go. I decided it was okay because I wouldn't actually have to touch it. I washed my hands, leaving them wet, unwilling to touch the towel.

"You about done in there?" Riley said as he ripped open the door.

"I guess I am now."

"Took you long enough," Riley snapped at me, and I wondered where the sudden hostility came from.

"If you say so."

"Hold out your hands," he ordered.

"Come on, seriously?" For a second I contemplated escape but knowing there were at least ten large men downstairs it didn't seem realistic. It wasn't time yet; I needed to wait 'til the right moment.

Riley didn't wait for an answer; he pulled my arms and began to tie them.

"Hey!" I yelped as he tied the rope so tightly it bit into my wrists.

"I'm not taking any chances. I already put myself on the line several times for you tonight."

"I know, and I appreciate it."

"How much do you appreciate it?" he said with a smarmy grin. "You still owe me a favor you know."

I searched his face, hoping his words were meant as a joke but I found no hint of humor.

"Let's go in here." With a hand on my shoulder, Riley led me into a small bedroom at the back of the cabin, closing the door behind him before pushing me down on the bed. I looked out a dirty window and saw nothing but woods.

"We have some time; I figured there was no reason to bring you back downstairs when we can get to know each other better up here."

"Umm, does that thing work?" I nodded toward the ancient looking TV on a rickety stand in the corner of the room.

"Yeah, why, you want to watch TV?"

"It's something." Riley seemed like a half-decent, albeit creepy guy, but I didn't know how long I could trust him in a room alone with me. I needed to get his eyes off me so I could figure out a way to escape.

"Can't we do something more fun?" His eyes devoured me, and I was completely aware of how little I was wearing.

"How can we do anything if you don't untie my hands?" I pointed out, grasping at straws.

He smirked. "There's lots you can do without your hands."

He came to sit down next to me on the bed, and I cringed as he ran a finger over my lips and I realized exactly what he was implying.

"I've been awfully nice to you, haven't I? If it weren't for me, who knows what would be happening to you right now. I want you so bad, baby."

I tried to hold it together. "If you want me so bad, why are you going to let Trevor give me to the Blackwells?"

He frowned. "It's a lot of money."

"How much of the money will you get?"

"I know what you're trying to do, and it's not going to work."

"It's not?"

Riley wiped sweat from his brow. "No. Trevor's the pack leader; his word is final. I'm lucky he's not with you himself. Maybe he's waiting to take his turn later."

His turn? Bile rose in my throat.

"I still don't understand how the prince could let you leave his sight—if you were my girl, you'd never leave my room." He ran his hands over my legs again and I whimpered, things were getting intense.

"I'd like to do this better, but I won't get another chance."

I panicked as Riley undid his belt with one hand, his other hand like a vise around my arm. I tried to twist from his grasp, but I didn't get far.

"Please don't do this," I begged, hoping to get to that decent part of him that had surfaced earlier.

"I'm never going to have a chance to get with a girl like you again. I can't waste it." He moved on to his button and began to slide down his jeans.

Shaking uncontrollably, I tried to speak. "I'm sure you can get plenty of girls who actually want to be with you, don't do this."

He froze. "Who actually want to be with me? You saying you don't want to be with me?" He glared at me and I realized I had said the worst possible thing. "You want to be with me, baby, and I'll show you why." His hand that had been near my knee moved to my thigh and didn't show signs of stopping. I tensed.

The room shook and a huge crash reverberated. "What the hell?" Riley pulled his pants back on, removing his hand from my leg and releasing my arm.

Shouts followed by what sounded like animals howling filled the air.

Riley went to the door. "Stay right here, this isn't over." He slammed the door shut, and I heard a piece of furniture move into place outside the door.

I had no idea what was going on downstairs or outside, but I hoped that I could use the chaos to my advantage.

Waiting until I heard his footsteps retreating, I awkwardly maneuvered so I was kneeling on the bed. This put me at the right height to try to jimmy the window open, which was no easy task with my hands tied.

"Ouch!" I cried as the metal of the window frame cut into the skin of my wrist. Finally, the window moved upwards. I used the wall to move to standing and kicked out the screen. With only a moment's hesitation, I ducked and took a step out onto the roof, thankful there was an overhang. I looked down into the darkness, glad I was only one story up, and hoping I wouldn't kill myself in the descent.

With a deep breath I jumped for it, landing hard on one ankle before falling to my knees. Pulling myself up I winced. The pain in my ankle was incredible and my knees were bleeding.

Trying to ignore the inhuman noises filling the night, I fought through the pain and took off running. Thankfully, I was on the backside of the house and had quick access to the woods. I prayed no one had seen me jump. With no thought to where I was going other than knowing I was moving farther from the house, I stumbled through the dark. I would have been quite the sight for anyone watching me run with my legs and wrists covered in blood and wearing only a bra and panties.

I pushed myself to keep running but the pain got worse until I could barely keep going. Just as I contemplated resting, a searing pain shot through my leg and I was knocked down onto my knees again. I rolled over onto my back, coming face to face with a cougar.

Terrified, I started to scream when suddenly a blur flew in kicking the animal off me. As the blur slowed, I realized it was a winged figure covered in streaks of blood. Two cougars lunged for the Pteron, but he flung out his wings knocking both several feet away instantly. With a crack they knocked into a couple of trees. I flinched at the sound of the impact.

Without warning, I was jerked up from the ground. Arms wrapped around my waist. Unsure of who held me, I struggled afraid it was the mysterious Blackwell family.

"Cut that crap out!"

I was in so much pain and so overwhelmed that I didn't try to place the voice and continued to struggle. Soon, I felt us land. We were surrounded on all sides by deep forest.

"What the hell, Allie! Do you want to get us killed?" Jared shouted as he stepped away from me.

"Jared?" I took a few steps towards him, tears of relief and fear slipping down my face.

He opened his arms, pulling me against his chest, letting me cry.

Jared held me for a moment, running his hands down my back to comfort me. His movements were stilted and I guessed this kind of contact was unusual for him.

Regaining some semblance of composure, I removed my head from his chest.

"Are you okay?" His eyes searched mine while revealing layers of fear, anger, and concern. He carefully untied my hands.

He moved back a few steps and looked me over. "Damn Allie, you look like shit."

"Gee, thanks." Now that I was with Jared I allowed myself to breathe. I wrapped my arms around myself, trying to cover up.

"Did any of those brutes touch you?

I looked down at the open wounds on my leg. "Define touch?"

"You know exactly what I'm talking about."

"Then no. It uh, got close but it didn't happen."

"Thank god." Jared surprised me by pulling me to him again. It felt strange. This wasn't Jared. "Levi would have been destroyed." So that was it. I pulled away. Just the mention of his name brought out the anger in me.

"Don't even say his name."

"Why not? What the hell were you thinking leaving by yourself like that? You just took off. You didn't give Levi a chance to explain himself. You ran away before Hailey could even talk to you." Evidently, Jared's anger had returned as well.

"You can't seriously be asking me that! After what Levi did to me."

"You're the one who decided to sleep with him, it was your choice." He sneered, any semblance of the concern from moments earlier all but gone.

I slapped him across the face instinctively. "Shut up. I had no idea what it meant."

He touched his face where I hit him. "I just saved you. You get that, right?"

"I had it under control. Besides, if it weren't for Levi and the rest of you I wouldn't be in this situation.

"Under control? Have you looked at yourself?"

I resisted the urge to examine the extent of the damage.

"Not that I don't enjoy seeing you half naked, but you can't possibly tell me you had it handled."

"Just take me home."

Jared shook his head in frustration. "This isn't over. You'll have to talk to Levi and accept reality."

"Please, just take me home." As much as I didn't want to see our houseguests, I wanted my mom.

"Not a chance. You aren't safe outside New Orleans."

I shuddered at the thought of getting taken again. "Fine, then take me to the hotel. I am not going with you unless you promise to take me there."

"Then what are you going to do, just stay out here?"

"What are you going to do, tell Levi you left me out here?"

"Fine, but first we need to get you something warmer to wear." Jared moved behind me like he was ready to get us flying again.

I spun around, facing him. "Where are we going?"

"There's a Pteron cabin nearby. We have a man here."

"You just happen to have a cabin in the middle of nowhere?"

"We have homes everywhere, get used to it."

"I don't plan to."

Jared placed his hands roughly on my already sore arms. "We don't have time to argue, but what you need to understand is that you aren't safe. What happened back there can and will happen again if you try to run. It was one thing when only a few of us knew that Levi and you connected, but now everyone knows. Your life as you knew it is over, deal with it."

I shivered at his words, my fear returning as the adrenaline from the anger faded.

"Let's go." Jared wrapped his arms around me and took off. I closed my eyes tightly, too emotional to handle anything else.

Jared landed, still keeping me close to his body. I leaned into him, unable to put too much weight on my legs.

"Who's out there?" A voice broke through the night catching me off guard, preventing me from responding.

"It's Jared, Allen. I have her."

"Oh, thank goodness." An older man walked out of the shadows moving towards us. I tensed beside Jared. His eyes went wide as he looked at me.

"Don't worry, it's being taken care of." Jared answered an unasked question. "I need to get her something warm, I'll have to take her up high."

"What? I'm not flying with you again. Let's find my car." Even though I argued, I didn't try to fight when Jared picked me up and carried me inside the cabin. I didn't care how angry I was; I needed more clothing.

"I'll get your car," Allen answered.

"Great." Jared tossed something to Allen and as he caught it, I realized he had my car keys.

"Hey, where did you get those?"

"We found your purse at the Dairy Queen."

"How did you know it was there?"

"The GPS." He smirked, seeming more like the Jared I knew.

"You have a GPS tracker on my car?" I struggled against him until he put me back down.

224

"Of course we do. You are Levi's so we had to watch you."

"Oh, just shut up. You know what, I don't care."

Allen stared at me openmouthed before talking. "There is clothing in the bedroom through that doorway."

I limped over to where he pointed and headed back.

I was just pulling a sweater over my head when Jared walked in. "I found a parka for you, you should be fine."

"Do we really have to fly?"

"Yes! I never took you as being dumb. How many times do I have to tell you about the danger before you accept it? We have to get you back to New Orleans."

Maybe it was the exhaustion or the intensity in Jared's glare, but I nodded.

Allen looked at me warmly as we walked outside. "It was an honor to meet you. I only wish it were under better circumstances."

An honor? "Um, yeah you too."

As Jared got ready to take off, I asked about it quickly. "What was that about?"

"You haven't figured it out yet, huh? I would have thought those stupid pumas would have told you."

"Told me what?"

225

"That you're the newest member of the royal family."

Hearing it from Jared shocked me. "So it's true?"

He laughed. "Yes, it's true. Hold on Princess, it's going to get cold. You may not breathe much for a minute or so, but it will be over soon."

Jared took off. As we rose up, I watched billowing smoke snake its way up through the night sky as sounds of wounded animals filled the air. Something told me there was nothing left of the cabin.

Jared wasn't kidding about going high. My eyes were no match for the wind and I had to give up the fight to keep them open. I felt intense pressure and panicked as I realized I couldn't really breathe. Just as I thought I couldn't take anymore, we began to descend. My ears screamed at me, it was worse than a quick descent on a plane.

Jared landed on the balcony outside my room. "There will be someone out here all night, you're safe."

I nodded, wanting nothing more than to go inside. Jared knocked on the glass door. A girl I didn't recognize opened it. Jared walked in with me limping behind him.

"Who are you and what are you doing in my room?" I winced as I put too much weight on the cut up leg and turned ankle.

"It's all clear." She nodded to Jared. "I apologize if you don't like my presence. I will be out in the hall if you need me." The girl bowed her head slightly before leaving the room, closing the door behind her.

Jared took out his cell phone. "We're back, and Allie definitely needs to be checked out. Send Dr. Ellis up."

"Dr. Ellis?" I asked, taking a seat on the couch.

"Yeah, he's our doctor."

"But what's he going to think?"

Jared smiled slightly. "He's our doctor, he's seen a lot weirder than this."

A knock on the door interrupted us and Jared went to open it.

"She's over here," Jared said formally, leading in a gray haired man with an old-fashioned black doctor's bag. "Her leg got swiped by a cougar."

"Hi, Allie, I'm Dr. Ellis. May I take a look at your leg?"

"Yes." I looked at him, wondering if he was human.

"All right, this looks worse than it is. Evidently, he or she used the least force necessary on you. I'm sure it's painful but it should heal."

He applied a coat of some sort of cream and bandaged my leg. "Try to keep it clean and I'll leave a tube of this ointment for you. You should change the bandage once a day. Take some ibuprofen every eight hours and it should be healed up in a few weeks. Call me if you have a fever or any increased redness." He handed me a nondescript business card with just his name and a phone number."

"Thank you."

"You are very welcome. Rest up." He smiled, nodded to Jared, and left the room.

"You think you're okay here? There'll be guards outside your room and on the balcony all night," Jared explained.

"I'll be fine."

"Okay, you have my number right? Call if you need anything." He headed toward the door.

"Jared?" I called just before he closed the door.

"Yeah?"

"Thanks for saving me."

"Not a problem. I'm glad you're okay."

I made sure to lock the door behind him.

I pulled off my borrowed clothes and took a hot shower, not caring that the bandage would have to be changed. No amount of water and soap could wash off the dirtiness I felt. I slid down the wall to sit on the floor and cried harder than I ever had in my life.

As the water in the shower turned cold, I finally got up and limped out. Slipping into a tank and PJ pants and applying a fresh bandage, I went to sleep hoping that when I woke up it would all be just a really bad dream.

Nineteen

My stomach woke me up the next morning. I hadn't eaten anything since the few bites of ice cream. I wasn't sure if I would ever eat the horrible substance again. If it weren't for my stupid craving, I might already be back in New York.

Walking into the kitchenette, I poured myself some cereal before collapsing in a chair in the living area. I finished quickly, rinsed out my bowl and pushed back the blinds. A man was sitting in a chair on the balcony wearing sunglasses with a paper in front of him. He could have been any tourist. At least he knew how to blend in. Tugging on the ring, I had no idea what I was going to do.

A knock on the door startled me from my thoughts. I ignored it but the knocking only got more intense.

"Allie, it's Owen, open up please."

"Go away; I don't want to talk to any of you."

Things got quiet and I thought he had left before a lighter knocking resumed.

"I said go away!"

"Allie, it's me," Hailey called out. "Please open up."

A part of me refused to believe she was in on all of this. If anyone was going to help me make sense of things it would be her.

"He isn't with you, is he?" I didn't even want to mention his name.

"No, I told him he'd only make things worse. And okay, he's being physically restrained, but either way he's not here."

I decided to trust her and reluctantly opened the door.

Returning to my seat on the couch, I pulled my knees up against my chest.

"Nice pjs," Owen joked. I guess opening the door to Hailey gave him an invitation as well.

"Shut up, Owen," Hailey snapped.

I laughed despite myself. "Are you seriously going to come in here and make fun of what I'm wearing after everything that's happened?"

"No, sorry. I honestly don't know what to say. Jared told us... He said you were in rough shape and weren't exactly dressed..."

"Stop, I'm not talking about it with you!" I let out the anger that felt ready to boil over.

"Okay. I get it. I wanted to make sure you realized you were safe now. You're safe here."

"What if I don't want to stay?"

"You don't have a choice," Owen said calmly, with no hint of the seriousness of what he was saying.

"Jared told me that, but why? Can you really guarantee I'm safe? Besides, can't someone reverse things and take off this damn ring?" I struggled once again to pull it off.

"Don't waste your energy, it's not budging. And you are safer here, where we can protect you,"

Owen said. "Besides, to answer your question, no one can reverse it. Levi chose you, and you agreed, so it's a done deal."

"I didn't agree to anything." I felt my temper rising.

"Maybe not with words but—"

"Don't go there Owen. Just don't," I warned.

"It wasn't fair of him. I'm not going to sit here and defend him." Owen cracked his knuckles.

"You better not!" Hailey fumed. "Levi can be such an idiot and jerk sometimes, or okay most of the time. But this is his biggest mess yet."

"If it helps any, he did it because he cares about you," Owen said.

"You've got to be kidding me."

"I can't believe I'm saying this but it's true. Levi wouldn't have done it if he didn't care. He tied himself to you as much as he tied you to him," Hailey said lightly.

"What do you mean he's tied to me? I still don't understand it."

"He can't be with anyone else now that he's given you the ring."

"Oh, come on! If that's true why did he do it? We barely know each other!"

"Honestly?" Owen asked, pausing to look out the window. "He was afraid."

"Afraid of what?"

231

"Of how he would feel when the inevitable happened and you left at the end of the summer. He was afraid of losing you."

"That's ridiculous. We were just having fun."

"No, it was more than that. Levi is crazy about you; he has been since he first met you. Then you challenged him and it just made things worse."

"So where does that leave me? I can't stay here forever."

"Would it really be that bad to stay in New Orleans longer? Forgetting about Levi for a second, you're not safe away from here. Do you really want to risk it?" Hailey asked carefully.

"My life isn't here."

"Not to be a bitch, Allie, but where is your life exactly?" Hailey sat down next to me. "I mean, what's waiting for you up north? An ex-boyfriend who doesn't get what over means and a college you are only going to for your parents?"

"My mom is up there!" I argued even as Hailey's words rang true. So much had changed, especially now that I knew about Mom's boyfriend moving in.

"You're leaving home either way. What's the difference between a two-hour drive and a two-hour flight? Both ways you're not at home."

When I didn't respond, Hailey placed a gentle hand on my arm. "Look, I'm sorry I said that. I was out of line, but I don't think staying here would be the worst thing for you, and besides I want you to stay."

232

"Owen, can I talk to Hailey alone?" I asked, even though I was prepared to kick him out if necessary. There was so much I wanted to say but not in front of Levi's friend.

"Well, I told Levi I would report back to him about—"

"Just leave, Owen. Who cares what Levi wants, this is about Allie." Hailey got up and started pushing him towards the door.

"Fine, but I'll be down the hall," he relented and walked out, closing the door behind him.

Hailey took her seat next to me again, sitting cross-legged. "I can't imagine what you went through."

The sincerity in Hailey's words matched the emotion in her eyes. Even as I struggled to understand the situation, I knew she was a friend and had no role in Levi's deception. Our friendship, as new as it was, was one of the only solid things I had to hold onto.

"It was horrible. The way he touched me... If we hadn't been interrupted..." I couldn't finish the thought. "I've never been so scared in my life."

"I'm so sorry."

"And the worst part is that even though it's over, I still feel so dirty. I can still feel the guy's hands all over me, and when I close my eyes I see his face. I've never felt so helpless before." I bet a million self-defense classes wouldn't have saved me, but I planned to sign up for one the first chance I got.

"I wish there was some way for me to erase what happened, but I know I can't. All I can do is promise you that I will never let that happen to you again. None of us will."

"I think that's why I'm tempted to stay. I'm afraid to leave." The thought of ever being in that situation again terrified me. I hated having to rely on others, but at this point, I had no choice.

"Will you at least consider it?"

"Staying?" I asked.

"Yeah."

"I'll think about it." The words flew out of my mouth before I could stop them. "But let's stop talking about what happened. I can't handle it."

"Really? You might stay?" Hailey's face lit up and she hugged me. "It's going to be so awesome; we'll be roommates and get to hang out all the time."

"Whoa, slow down. First of all, I said I'd think about it, not that I'd do it. Secondly, in case you forgot, I'm not enrolled at Tulane, and lastly, you already have a roommate."

"If you're thinking about it, you are going to do it. Anyway, be realistic, between our connections, money, and your ridiculous academic background are you really worried about getting in?"

"My ridiculous academic background?"

"You're supposed to go to Princeton. Don't tell me you don't have perfect SATs and grades."

"Well, what about your roommate?"

234

"What about her? You think I want to live with that girl? Besides, getting things changed will be easy. All I have to do is tell my dad about her panties on the door plan and it's a done deal."

Talking to Hailey about living together got me excited. If I was being honest with myself, Levi aside, I didn't want to leave New Orleans. Even without the fear for my safety, I would have been tempted to stay.

"Like I said, I'll think about it."

"You do realize what you still have to do though?" she asked, avoiding my eyes.

"What?"

"You have to talk to Levi."

"Why? Just because I stay doesn't mean I'm going to be with him."

"Well, then you can tell him that. He's not going to back down until you two talk things out."

"Lovely. Will you come with me? I don't trust myself to refrain from slugging him."

Hailey laughed. "You ready then?"

"Now?" I asked alarmed.

"What time were you thinking?"

"Never…"

"Exactly. Let's go, the sooner the better." She tugged on my arm to pull me up from my seat.

"At least let me get changed. If I'm facing him I'm not doing it in this." I gestured to my pajamas.

I didn't wait for a response and walked into my room to change. I pulled on a pair of jeans and a t-shirt because I wanted to cover up my bruised up knees and my bandaged leg. Hopefully, no one noticed my wrists. I was bound to run into someone, and I didn't want any extra questions. Natalie knew what happened, but no one else did.

***

Levi leaned against the window at the front of the corner coffee shop. He didn't notice us approaching, and he looked way too good. If I thought I could avoid thinking about the last time we were together, I was totally delusional.

"Hey man," Owen called out. He flanked me with Hailey on my other side, both helping take some weight off my bad leg. The several times I attempted to turn around, the two of them had me facing forward again. I knew that avoiding this confrontation was pointless but it didn't mean I wanted it.

Levi looked up, locking eyes with me immediately. He took two steps forward reaching toward me. I fought the urge to take his hand and he got the hint lowering his arm.

We stood there looking at each other for a moment before he took another step toward me, pulling me into his arms. I wanted to struggle, but I didn't. As angry and hurt as I was, there was something so safe about those arms that I needed to be there for a moment.

"I'm so glad you're safe," he whispered.

Before I could start crying, I pulled away.

"Okay, so we're going to get going..." Hailey said trailing off. "Come on, Owen."

"Oh yeah. Bye," Owen said.

I turned to shoot Hailey a dirty look but she was already disappearing down the street.

"You want to go inside?" Levi asked awkwardly.

"Sure."

He held open the door for me and we walked up to the counter. "One large coffee," I ordered without waiting for Levi.

"Make that two." Levi handed a card to the barista.

I took my coffee, adding two Splendas and no cream and sat down at a table by the window. Levi was two steps behind me.

My eyes remained focused on the table as I heard the scrape of a chair across from me.

"If it changes anything, I didn't mean to upset you."

My head snapped up to attention immediately. "What?"

"I didn't want to hurt you." Levi reached his hand across the table to touch mine, but I jerked it away.

"Then what did you want exactly?"

"You." His eyes bore into mine as he spoke.

"Clever, very clever."

237

"It's the truth. You asked why I did it and that's the honest answer. I did it because I wanted you."

"What part of wanting me required you to trick me into entering into some weird relationship?"

"Weird relationship? Is that what you think this is?"

"What am I supposed to think it is?"

"There is nothing weird about it, most girls would be happy to find out they've become a princess."

"I guess I'm not like most girls. And what is with all this princess talk? When were you going to tell me you were the future king or whatever it is they call you exactly?"

"It didn't seem important before... and I didn't want to scare you off."

I laughed dryly. "Well, you did a pretty good job with that."

"It wasn't supposed to be like this."

"No? What was it supposed to be like? Am I supposed to fawn at your feet thanking you for picking me? Dream on."

"Damn it, don't be so difficult. You were there that night; we work so well together. It's amazing. Can't that be enough?"

"You have that much confidence in your sexual prowess to think that means anything?"

"I am not talking about me, I'm talking about us."

"There is no *us*. Whatever chance we had is gone. You tricked me, lied to me, used me and pretty much did anything you possibly could to destroy us." I twisted my hands in my lap. "You're the reason I was kidnapped and nearly raped. It's your fault." I looked down, unwilling to let him see how much I hurt.

"I am so sorry. Words can't even describe it. The thought of those brutes touching you…" He gripped the table, his knuckles turning white. "I promise you they will never bother you or anyone else again." He scooted his chair next to me. "Please, give me a chance to make it up to you." There was nothing natural about Levi pleading.

I looked up at him with tear-rimmed eyes. "The only thing I want is an explanation. Why me? Why in the world did you pick me? You hardly know me."

"I've never felt this way about anyone before. Usually I get tired of a girl after a few days, but you, I'll never get tired of you. You challenge me and it only makes me want you more. I know you feel it too. Don't bother denying it. The physical pull between us is undeniable."

"That's what this is all about? You're physically attracted to me? I still don't see how that makes me different."

"Doesn't the thought of being together excite you at all? You seemed so interested in my world, so caught up in it. Can't that be enough for now?"

Glancing around, I noticed a few people staring at us so I lowered my voice. "Levi, are you even listening to me? Do you really expect me to forgive you for what you put me through? You make it sound like you stood me up."

"I'm sorry baby, I'm sorry. You were only kidnapped because you ran off. I didn't expect you to do that. I already planned to explain more over dinner. Remember, I told you I had something important to tell you." He leaned over the table.

"Don't you ever call me baby. Do you hear me? Never!" Hearing it made me think of Riley and his dirty, wandering hands.

"Okay. I won't. I'm sorry." He picked up one of my hands, examining the cuts and bruises on my wrist. I pulled it out of his reach. "I'm so sorry."

I took a deep breath. "Didn't you think I'd try to take the ring off?"

Levi shrugged. "I never really thought about it."

"Exactly!" I yelled exasperated. Standing up, I called over my shoulder, "You didn't think and look where it got us."

Dropping my half-empty coffee cup in the garbage, I pushed open the door. I didn't have to turn around to realize Levi was at my heels.

"Wait up!" He grabbed my arm pulling me towards him.

"Let go of me!"

"You don't understand how important this is. You can't just walk away from me. You have to be with me now."

"I don't have to do anything."

"Give me a chance to explain more, to show you."

"I gave you that chance inside." I gestured to the door we just walked through.

"Let me show you more of my people, introduce you, make you see how important you are."

"Why would I do that?"

"Because you're a good person. Because even if you hate me, you don't hate Hailey and you sure as hell don't hate the city of New Orleans."

"Why would being together affect New Orleans?"

"It means everything. Without you, my family's reign ends and the headquarters likely moves— taking everything with it. Do you really want to see New Orleans robbed of more? Like Katrina wasn't enough."

"Shut up!" Well aware of people watching us I continued. "Don't compare me leaving to a hurricane!"

"There is so much you don't understand. New Orleans needs us. Please let me show you. If you still don't want anything to do with us afterwards, we'll figure something else out, but at least give me one night to prove it to you."

"One night?"

"Yes. Just one night."

"Fine. One night and then you find a way to let me leave."

Levi smiled slightly with relief. "Good."

We walked the rest of the way back to the hotel in silence. I hobbled painfully but refused Levi's attempts to help me. I knew that he kept looking over at me but I avoided his eyes, I was afraid of what effect it would have on me. I already had to fight the urge to slip my hand into his. He wasn't exaggerating the physical attraction.

About to head to the front entrance, I stopped when Levi called my name. "I'll see you soon, I'll have Hailey give you all the details."

"Details? What kind of night is this?"

Levi smiled broadly. "Just wait and see. All I'll tell you is that it's a party." He took advantage of my surprise to kiss me lightly on the cheek before walking away.

Twenty

"I won't even ask how you got into my room without me." Pushing the door closed behind me, I immediately noticed Hailey sprawled out on my couch.

"So how'd it go?" Hailey asked. She put aside her copy of People magazine. Hailey really had such a weakness for celebrity gossip.

"Do you even need to ask?"

"It couldn't have been that bad, right?"

"He said he needed one night to convince me to stay. After that, if I want to leave he'll find a way to make it happen."

"One night? Did he mention which night?"

"He told me you would give me the details but that it's a party."

"Oh." Hailey seemed to be contemplating what I said for a minute. "Oh! I bet I know what he's thinking."

"What?"

"Hmm, I need to find out for sure. I'll be back." Hailey got up and headed to the door.

"Great."

As I waited for Hailey to get back, I decided to call Dad. I hadn't checked in with him since the dinner with Levi and thought I should at least try. The call went to voicemail after a few rings. I thought about calling my mom, but I didn't know what to tell her until I had a better idea of my new plans.

Hailey was gone longer than I expected. I turned on the TV, but daytime channel surfing can only keep you busy for so long.

Right as I was about to give up and head down to the lobby, Hailey burst back into my room. "I was right. You need a dress."

I turned off the TV. "Excuse me? I have plenty of dresses. What did you have in mind?"

Hailey was already one step ahead of me. She ran into my room, and I followed her. She quickly flipped through my dresses in the closet. "Okay, nothing works."

"What do you mean? What's wrong with what I have?"

"They're not formal enough," she explained.

"Formal? What kind of party is this?" I walked back out to crash on the couch.

"Okay, promise you won't get upset."

"Not a chance I'm promising that."

Hailey cracked a small smile. "Okay, I figured that much, so at least promise not to be upset with me."

"Fine. I'll save my anger for Levi."

"Well, it's kind of like an engagement party."

"An engagement party? Why would that upset me?" Then I thought about what she was saying. "Hold on, whose engagement party?"

"Yours." She looked down at the ground.

"No way. No freaking way."

"Remember, no taking it out on me."

"Levi has to be the most infuriating man on the planet. He tells me to give him one night like it's nothing, and it's an engagement party!"

"It's not exactly an engagement party because you guys are more than engaged, but you get the idea."

"You don't actually think I'm going to this, right?"

"I know it seems awful, but what other choice do you have?"

"I should just leave."

"Yeah and get kidnapped again? Levi has lots of bad traits but he does keep his word. If he says that he'll find a way for you to leave afterwards, then he's serious. Why not suck it up and do it? If by the end of the night, you're not convinced then it's over."

"Does this mean we're going shopping?" I asked.

"Yes! It's going to be so much fun."

Hailey's celebration was cut short as her cell phone rang. "Hello? Oh, hi. Sure, I'll ask her."

"Who's that?" I mouthed.

"I'll have to call you back." She hung up the phone.

"How do you feel about meeting Levi's mom?"

"Why would I want to do that?"

"Because she's downstairs waiting to come up to talk to you. She's really a nice woman. Too bad she didn't rub off on Levi enough."

"She's downstairs now?" I gasped.

"Yeah. Should I call back and tell her to come up?"

"Do I really have a choice?"

"Probably not."

"All right then." This kept getting worse.

I went to the bathroom to splash water on my face as I waited for Hailey to return the phone call. Looking at myself in the mirror, I cringed. Exhaustion wasn't a good look on me.

A light rap on the door let me know she had arrived. Hailey got the door while I smoothed out my t-shirt. For some insane reason I cared about what she thought of me.

A beautiful and petite brunette walked in. "Hailey, would you give us some time?"

"Sure, Mrs. Laurent." Hailey gave me an apologetic look before slipping out of the room.

I stepped towards her and held out a hand. "It's nice to meet you Mrs. Laurent."

She shook my hand lightly before pulling me in for a hug. "Call me Helen. We're going to be family after all."

I stiffened and pulled away.

246

"Why don't we sit down?" she suggested, taking a seat on one side of the couch. I sat down on the other side and looked at her.

"Helen, I appreciate you taking the time to speak with me, but I don't know if you are aware of what is actually going on with me and your son."

"You mean he didn't trick you into entering into a bonding you were unaware of?"

"Well, yes," I admitted.

"I am well aware of what my birdbrain of a son did to you."

I tried not to laugh at the use of the term "birdbrain." How fitting.

"I'm not here to defend him. I only want to tell you my story and maybe answer some of your questions. I am sure you have plenty."

She was right, I had tons of questions and she seemed harmless enough. "All right."

"You aren't the first human woman to fall victim to a Pteron royal." She paused, looking to make sure I followed. "I was a few years older than you when it happened, but I trust the experience wasn't too different."

"Okay." She had me intrigued.

"I'm not sure what you have been told, but you are incredibly important to our people now."

"I gathered that, but how so?"

Helen lifted her left hand revealing an identical ruby ring. "Each heir to the throne gets one of these rings. Once the ring is given and the

247

relationship consummated he can never be with another."

"What do you mean, can't be with another? What's to stop him?"

"Honor. Power. The knowledge that New Orleans would suffer another great hardship."

"I don't follow."

"Our family only retains power if we continue to have an heir. An heir can only be born from the king, or future king, and his mate. The ring marks the mate, which is why the ring can never be removed. If Levi steps out on you in the slightest, he forfeits it all."

"But what does this have to do with hurting New Orleans?"

"If our family loses control, the seat of power moves to where the next leading family lives. If the seat moves so does the entire base of the supernatural community. We're talking a lot of money and influence—things our city can't afford to lose. "

"You're trying to tell me that if I don't have an heir with Levi, the power structure changes completely?"

"Yes. Of course, no one is expecting you to have a child now. It's enough that there is a potential. Levi's father and I were together for years before having him."

"Oh, but what if you, well, what if you couldn't have a child?"

"If a woman wasn't able to carry a Pteron child for him he wouldn't select her. It's a simple matter of survival instinct."

I didn't think there was anything simple about it. The conversation was making me sick. I didn't like being in the same room with Levi, so talking about having a baby with him was way too much.

"I know this is all a lot to take in, but you must remember that you don't have to act on anything immediately. We are only asking you to stay in the city so we can keep you safe and to keep up appearances."

Wow. Talk about bluntness. "Keep up appearances?"

"I realize how that must sound to you, but it's essential that we don't set off any panic. If anyone were to think a power shift was possible, it could set off a war or worse. Trust me, it wouldn't be pretty."

I didn't dare ask what could be worse than a war.

"So you want me to stay in New Orleans and pretend to be your son's girlfriend?"

"I'd rather you not pretend, but maybe the two of you just need time. I believe that eventually you will forgive him and realize how right you are for each other. You wouldn't have been drawn to each other if you weren't. Not to mention that he needs you. He needs a woman who will stand up to him and force him to be the best man he can be."

"You make it sound so easy, like it's nothing."

"I certainly don't mean to. I only want to spare you from repeating my own mistakes."

"What do you mean?"

"I wasn't tricked the way you were, but I still didn't understand. Robert told me that intimacy after accepting the ring would bind us forever, but I didn't really think about what forever meant. When we got into our first fight, I rushed out of the city back to my family home, much as you tried to do. Only, I lived closer and I actually arrived." Helen looked wistful.

"What happened?"

"Suffice to say I was followed back and my sister was the one to pay. But that's a story for another day."

Noting the sadness on Helen's face, I didn't press for more details, but I could tell the story didn't have a happy ending. I hadn't even considered that my family could be at risk. How could I leave my mom vulnerable? It felt like the walls were closing in on me.

"Like it or not, you are part of this world now. You can't run from it, whether you want to or not."

"But Levi said I could leave. He said if I wasn't convinced after the party—"

"I know what he said and he means it, but it doesn't mean your actions won't have repercussions."

"Have you ever felt like your life was just a series of mistakes?"

"Sure I have. I think that's what we call growing up. But sweetie, we aren't defined by the mistakes we make, but by what we learn from those mistakes and how we move on."

Words stopped on the tip of my tongue, what if we don't know how to move on? I kept the thought to myself.

"I'm glad you came here." Talking to Helen gave me an insight I doubt anyone else could have and it gave me more to think about, especially when it came to protecting my family.

"I'm glad too. I know things seem bleak now, but it will all work out. In some ways, you are saying goodbye to your old life, or maybe just the life you planned to live, but in turn, you are getting a new one. You have the chance to be something great, and make a big difference. Not too many people get that opportunity." Helen patted my knee lightly. "Now, I should let you get some rest."

"Rest?"

"Thursday is going to be a big day."

"This Thursday?"

"Yes. The party isn't until the evening, but there will be a whole day of preparation before."

"Preparation?" I asked.

"Relax. I'm talking about a spa day."

"Oh. I guess I also need to shop."

"I wouldn't worry about that. I already found the perfect dress for you. I'll have it sent over later." She smiled.

"How do you know my size?"

"Levi has an eye for sizes."

"Why doesn't that surprise me?" I groaned, wondering how many other girls he had "sized."

"I wouldn't let it get to you. You are the only girl that will ever matter to him now."

"I'm the one that doesn't want to be with him, remember?"

"Yes, I remember." She winked before heading to the door.

"I'll see you then."

"Bye."

Twenty-One

I shouldn't have worn stiletto heels. The thought catapulted through my mind as I navigated the lawn on my way to the opulent white tent. To be fair, Hailey and Helen had told me the party was outside, but the silver heels looked perfect with the floor length red dress Helen had sent over for me. The dress fit flawlessly, and I wasn't thrilled that Levi was able to pinpoint my size so precisely. It seemed somehow too intimate—even though he had every reason to know intimate details about me. I probably wouldn't have picked out a sweetheart neckline myself, but it worked perfectly with a single strand of pearls. The back dipped just enough and as uncomfortable as I was about the whole idea of the party, I knew that I looked good.

When the black limo picked me up earlier that evening, I half expected Levi to be waiting for me inside. I tried to ignore the wave of disappointment that hit me when I noticed the empty interior. Hailey explained that they all had to go to some meeting beforehand, but it surprised me that they made me go alone.

I've always been a firm believer in the concept of being fashionably late, but that description didn't fit what waited for me when I finally reached the tent. Clutching my evening bag, I plastered on a confident smile and walked inside.

The outside of the tent had been deceptively small for the space inside was twice as big. Tables lined the exterior while a large dance floor took up the middle. A giant skylight provided an incredible view of the night sky, only accentuated by the crystal chandeliers anchored from the ceiling of the tent.

The loud chatter of the crowd died down as I surveyed the sea of white and black in front of me. I was going to kill Helen and Hailey. My red dress stood out like a beacon in a dark sky.

Levi walked over to me swiftly, his eyes never leaving me. Placing his glass on a table, he left a man standing there mid-conversation. I tried to ignore how handsome he looked in his black tux.

"You look amazing." The expression on Levi's face spoke volumes louder than his words. Despite my anger, I was glad he approved.

"Thank you." I refused to let him know his approval mattered. I tried to look around disinterestedly but had to snap at him anyway. "Was the red dress really necessary?"

"Absolutely. Red is definitely your color by the way."

"You can give it up, Levi. Flattery isn't going to get you anywhere."

He shrugged. "I'm just speaking the truth. Did you have any trouble getting here? The car came on time and everything?"

"Everything was fine," I said tersely, not in the mood to make small talk.

"I'm sorry I couldn't bring you myself."

"Hailey explained why *she* couldn't come." I spoke quietly, careful to avoid being overheard. I didn't want to break my end of the bargain. I had promised Helen I would give this a fair shot and try not to make my reluctance too obvious.

Levi's slightly wounded expression surprised me. I didn't think he was capable of really being affected by anyone's opinion of him.

"I'm glad you're here."

"It's beautiful."

"Not as beautiful as you." I would have written off Levi's corny line if I hadn't seen his look of complete adoration.

"Is Hailey here?" I asked glancing around. The crowd was mostly older than we were, and I could have sworn I recognized a few faces. "Wait, isn't that the Governor of Louisiana?"

"Yeah, that's Bobby," Levi said nonchalantly. "Remind me to introduce you later."

"Is that Hailey over there?" My original question was answered when she waved at me. With her long hair pulled up into an elaborate updo, I almost didn't recognize her.

"We can go talk to her in a minute. Do you mind if we talk to my parents first?"

I nodded.

Levi took my arm leading me toward his mother and a man I assumed was his father. I studied him as we walked over; searching for evidence that he was any sort of king. He looked like an older version of Levi, his hair a striking shade of grey that made him look stately rather than old.

"Allie, you look breathtaking." Helen embraced me warmly.

"Thank you, Helen. You look wonderful as well." I turned on cocktail party mode, willing myself to pretend this was just another function for my dad.

"Ah, Allison, my son didn't exaggerate your beauty after all," his father said with a broad smile.

I dismissed the urge to correct him on the use of my full name. "It's nice to meet you, Mr. Laurent."

"It's just Robert. I suppose you could also call me Dad if you wanted, since you'll be my daughter-in-law soon." He beamed.

Warning bells went off in my head and both Helen and Levi looked at me pleadingly. Robert had no idea what was really going on with Levi and I. I smiled weakly, confident that this would be an extremely inopportune time to make a scene. "I think I'll use Robert."

"Fair enough. Levi tells me you two aren't going to be rushing into a formal wedding. I understand your father's concern with how young you are, but I'd be happy to talk to him for you. I look forward to meeting him sometime soon."

As I listened to this jovial man go on about meeting my father, I knew I needed to make an exit. "It was wonderful to meet you, but Levi, would you mind stepping outside with me for a moment? I could use some fresh air."

"Of course, sweetheart," Levi answered quickly clasping my hand in his.

"We'll be right back," Levi said quickly, like he was afraid I would start screaming if he didn't get me outside fast enough. He was right.

Once again, my choice of shoe attire frustrated me as we walked a distance from the tent to talk. My injuries were healing well, but it probably would have been smarter to wear flats.

"What the heck, Levi? Your dad thinks I've agreed to marry you?"

"Look, I know you're mad but with my dad there was no choice. He would have gone crazy if I told him the truth, and trust me it wouldn't have helped you at all."

"What are you talking about? All it would mean is us not playing this little game here. Like we're fooling anyone."

"Lower your voice. Seriously, if my dad finds out the truth we're both in trouble."

"What's he going to do to me?"

"My dad is in charge of the entire paranormal community and you doubt he could do something to you?"

"I'm just a human. He can't hurt me."

"First of all, you are not just a human. You are my mate. Big difference, and he could force you to marry me tonight if he wanted to."

"What are you talking about?"

"Like I said my dad has his ways. Let's stop this. You promised to give tonight a chance. Please, won't you at least try?"

"Okay."

"Are you ready to go back in?"

"Sure."

We walked back into the tent to the sound of clinking as several people tried to silence the crowd. Robert strode purposely to the center of the dance floor.

"Thank you everyone for being with us tonight. It isn't often that we have the pleasure of welcoming so many members of the community to our home, and we are so thankful that you were able to join us on this happy occasion. Many of you probably thought this day would never come." Polite laughter made Robert pause.

"I am well aware of my son's reputation with women, but it seems he has met his match. I have never seen Levi so happy or focused, and I know that we can expect great things from him as he formally takes his position next year. On that note, it's my pleasure to introduce you to Allison Davis, Levi's beautiful mate."

Levi steered us over to his dad. "Thank you father. You're right. I have met my match, and she's my match in every sense of the word. I have no doubt you will all learn to adore her as much as I do. Our community is new to her, but I am sure she will make a seamless transition. Now sweetheart, will you give me this dance?"

I nodded.

A quartet struck up a beautiful ballad and loud applause filled the tent as Levi led me onto the dance floor. I tried to ignore the shiver creeping down my back from his touch and the way he looked at me as though I were the only one in the room.

Levi took a slight bow, gesturing for me to do the same. I followed his lead, and we started to dance. Dancing with Levi was as natural as you would expect, but the closeness unnerved me. I didn't want to want him so much.

The song came to an end, but the quartet started another slow tune without a break.

Taking advantage of the slower music, he started talking quietly. "Al, I'm sorry. I'd do anything to erase what happened to you. I messed up, I know I did but I also know that there is something real between us."

"I don't see how you expect me to believe that."

"Please. It's true. We have to at least give this a chance," he pleaded.

"So, what, I throw away all my plans?"

"Defer Princeton until the spring. One semester at Tulane won't hurt; you'll probably like it. We can make sure you're roommates with Hailey and everything."

"If I agree, it's only for a semester."

"So you'll give us a chance?"

"This isn't about you and me. This is about New Orleans and keeping myself and my family safe. I'll stay, but you need to accept that we're not really together." I knew in my heart I couldn't leave. If what everyone was telling me was true, I might end up causing even more heartache to a city that had already been through so much. I also refused to put my parents or friends in danger, especially considering there was a part of me that was excited about spending a few more months in New Orleans—giving myself more time to experience something new.

Levi pulled me tightly against him. "I love you. I have never felt this way before and the thought of losing you scares me."

"And that's supposed to make everything better?" I bristled. "You love me? It doesn't matter anyway."

"Why not?"

"Because I don't love you." Even as the words left my lips, I knew they weren't true.

Made in the USA
San Bernardino, CA
02 December 2013